THE SHAMETOWN SAGA

The Shametown Saga

Andrew Hobgood

Cap and Glasses Studios

ISBN: 979-8-9880098-2-5 (Paperback)
ISBN: 979-8-9880098-1-8 (Hardcover)
ISBN: 979-8-9880098-0-1 (Digital)

Library of Congress Control Number: 2023910477

Front cover image by Joe Lino.

Printed in the United States of America.

First Printing 2024.

Cap and Glasses Inc
Milwaukee, WI 53204

www.capandglasses.com
www.AndyWritesThings.com

Dedicated to my parents
Patricia and Charles.

Who always encouraged me
to be who I am and make my weird art
no matter what.

Contents

PART TWO
ONE YEAR AGO

INTRODUCTION

Okay. Here's where things stand right now:

If you look to your right, you can see an old wooden fence on that hill. In just a moment, the road takes us up that way. And our destination awaits just beyond the hill and forty miles down a single-lane dirt road.

Ralph Elmore's crew won't allow us to get all the way down the road - they blocked it off about a half-mile from the gate. But it's not what lays beyond the gate I brought you here to show you. I want you to see what that old fuck Elmore has been up to.

Now, you want to concentrate on this next stretch of "road" - it rained last night, and nobody around here drives a Camry, so they have no incentive to make this mud pit drivable. The name of the game here is Don't Get Stuck. Your best bet is to follow in the tire tracks of their pickups and ATVs at a steady 15 MPH.

Based on the freshness of some of these tracks, you can tell some supplies or new recruits - probably both - arrived sometime in the last eight or nine hours.

This isn't going to be an amicable interaction, by the way. The guys at the roadblock are there because they are huge assholes. Intimidation is better than violence. Broken noses and bullet wounds tend to draw the police's attention. Nobody wants that. Ralph, least of all. He is five months past due on child support.

The standoff at the gate is already in its second week. But nobody outside this side of Montana has noticed.

That's because most people don't even realize what is going on.

I don't know if Ralph intended for this to get so big. Honestly, I don't know if he even knew what would happen.

But it all started when he and his former brothers-in-law - Ray, Rayray, Dickie, and Bart - decided to shut down the influx of out-of-towners.

"They're gonna take over. We'll be just like Illinois," Rayray fumed over a High Life one night down at Don's bar - which Don had named Don's. Don's was open whenever anyone wanted it to be - Don lived above the bar, so all you had to do was ring his doorbell, and he'd let you in. Good ol' Don.

"They're building their own fucking Chicago. Gonna start controlling the vote," Rayray continued.

Rayray was by far - by far - the most politically well-read of the group. Growing up, he was always sort of on his own. He took to reading books - he always kept paperbacks in the back pocket of his work jeans and would try to do all his chores as fast as possible so he could lay in one of the stables and catch up with Sherlock and Watson. He rarely spoke about the books or mysteries he was trying to solve because it would only result in being called a faggot.

Rayray's mother, JulieAnne, was his father's second wife. His father, Dick, lost his first wife in childbirth with Rayray's older brother Ray. Both of Dick's wives had wanted to name their firstborn sons after their fathers - both of whom shared the name Ray. But, of course, Dick already had a son named Ray. So when the birth certificate was being filled out, they named him Ray Mulford II. The original plan was to call the older son Ray and the newborn "Ray 2" or "Ray Too" - but his grandmother instead set the precedent of calling him Rayray because "he's twice the Ray," she used to sing to him.

Following Ray and Rayray, the Mulfords decided to name their third child after Dick, resulting in the given-name Dickie.

I don't know where the name Bart came from. Neither do JulieAnne or Dick. It was just something they picked out of thin air when they begrudgingly had to name an unexpected fifth child.

Their fourth child was a daughter - which was the only reason they had a fourth child. Dick was pretty satisfied with three boys, but JulieAnne had always wanted a daughter. So following the birth of JuliEtta, JulieAnne and Dick had their respective organs sewn and snipped to avoid any more than the planned four.

JuliEtta was Ralph's first and only wife. Ralph had never liked city folk, but his distaste only grew after her cancer diagnosis. He took her to all of the best hospitals in the most expensive cities - all of which were his first and only visits to the urban metropolises of America. The doctors talked and moved too quickly - compared to their doctor at home - and always seemed to be rushing them out of their hair. The breakneck pace of these city hospitals confused and irritated Ralph. He felt like they just didn't give a shit. Why would some prominent Memphis oncologist care about a poor woman from Montana?

After JuliEtta's death, her brother's' bond with Ralph only grew stronger. She had been the light of all their lives - and the loss should be shouldered by all five.

But old Ralph never forgave the "city dwellers" for how they treated them. And as he and Rayray - who was his age - started to spend more time together, he became obsessed with the unfairness of the growing urban dictatorship of the country. The fucking liberals and their bastions of excess and corruption were absconding government control. (He learned "absconding" from Rayray, whose vocabulary was well above average.) As Rayray said time and again, "all you have to do is look at Illinois!" Doesn't matter what the people want -

the assholes in Chicago make every decision that impacts the southern farmers in the state.

So when word floated to Bart about the two Chicagoans that had just bought themselves a ranch nearby, he immediately brought it to Ralph and his brothers' attentions. At first, no one cared too much.

Things didn't really begin to heat up until Bart filled up at the local gas station several weeks later. He got most of his gossip from Gerry, the hotdog bun of a man who owns the place and has worked the register every hour since opening - when he witnessed another pair of strangers moving to the old ranch. At least they hoped to move there, they said. The duo was an older Black woman - about 70, maybe - and her 12-year-old grandson. She held herself stately and tall, with a shock of gray running through her short curls. The boy had not yet begun his growth spurt, but you could already imagine him six inches taller than his grandmother within the year. He was darker than she was, thanks to his Nigerian father. He used to keep his head buzzed, but he started letting his hair grow naturally after his grandmother had to homeschool him.

Gerry had been trying to silently signal Bart to look up in the security mirror above his head so he, too, would see the strangers pulling bottles of water out of the cooler in the back of the shop. But before Bart could correctly interpret Gerry's gestures - the pair walked past him and up to the register.

Bart stood and listened as Gerry made small talk and tried to pry information out of them.

"Here for a visit?" he asked.

"Maybe longer."

"Got family nearby?"

"We are each other's family," she said, nodding to the boy.

"You hear about that ranch down the road?" he dug further, "A couple folks from Chicago bought it and moved in a few weeks ago."

"That's where we're headed," she answered matter-of-factly.

While she dug into her wallet for her bank card, Gerry gave Bart an eyebrows-raised look. After the strangers drove off, Bart proceeded to take that same look over to Don's, where he knew for sure Ralph would be smoking cigarettes and alternately sipping coffee and High Life.

That all happened about a year ago. Not quite a year, but close enough.

Now, if you pull over just before we get to the top of that hill just ahead of us, we can get out and see what the scene looks like without them noticing us. So I want you to take it all in while they're acting naturally.

As you can see, we're only about two miles from the gate - but from up here, you can start to make out some of the town in the distance. Unfortunately, however, the houses are all single-level, so you can't see many of those - and but the main farmhouse, old barns, and silos stand out clearly against the sunrise.

But it isn't the farmhouse, barns, or silos riling everyone up. It's the new houses. Rumor has it there are at least fifty on the property at this point. That doesn't bode well in the eyes of Ralph Elmore and crew.

The locals weren't concerned when it was just Rami and Brooke living in the farmhouse because "if they want to hole themselves up in the middle of nowhere, I don't see how it matters shit to me," as Ray put it. They weren't even worried when others started moving into the farmhouse. "'Less they start up a brothel in there, I don't care what they're doing long as they don't bother me with it," Don chimed in one night from behind lenses so thick they distorted his eyes when you looked at him, all five feet of him. (Everyone knows - but no one says it: Don put in a raised platform behind the bar so he can look his customers in the eye.) Of course, Dickie - as he's wont to do - thought he'd get a big laugh when he patted Don on the shoulder and shouted, "Better hope it's not a brothel - or you'll lose all your business!" Nobody really laughed, though. Not because it wasn't funny - but because of the stranger who had just walked into the bar.

He was a clean-shaven older gentleman with salt and pepper hair, dressed neatly in white slacks, a matching blazer, and a blue bow tie with pink polka dots. His crisp, white dress shirt stood out brightly against the muted earth tones of the other patrons. He was the whitest thing in the room.

"'scuse me, gentlemen. I'm trying to find..." He pulls out his cell phone and walks over to Derrick Hoover - who just happens to be sitting closest to the entrance. He holds his phone for Derrick to see and points, adding, "...this road here. I'm trying to get to Mr. Mahmoud's farmhouse - but couldn't find any signs with street names, and my GPS isn't getting a signal - "

"You're a friend of his?" Bart interrupted. This made the stranger freeze for a moment before recovering and answering, "I'm a doctor," which didn't get much of a response from Bart, who didn't really know what he meant, so he added, "Doctor-Patient confidentiality. You know." Bart still didn't know. But nodded anyhow.

Derrick broke the awkwardness by taking the man's phone away and swiping the screen. "We're here," he pointed and then handed the phone back.

The man felt the first sense of relief since he walked through the front door. When he entered and the room went silent, he was sure they all recognized him. But there were no knowing looks between the men at the bar and no mention of the video. He thought it best not to press his luck - the longer they were looking at him, the more likely his face would seem familiar to one of them - so he thanked them for their help and made a beeline out to the gravel parking lot.

After the door closed behind the stranger, no one said a word. Just silent, suspicious looks between the Montanans. At least, not until Ralph spoke up: "We should keep an eye on them."

That was all he needed to say. It was enough. And everyone nodded in agreement.

We should head back to the car. Better to make ourselves known first than for them to "catch us spying." If they think we're just gawkers, they won't harass us too severely. They'll make it clear you can't step past the barricade - but they won't touch you unless you do otherwise.

Go slowly. The locals know we're not from around here based on our car alone. If we approach too fast, they'll get anxious; assume we're making a move to drive through the fencing. Once one of them sees us - someone will wave you to a spot of their choosing, probably over on the grass. Just do what he says. Don't let his gun make you panic. He's not going to shoot you. You're not of concern to him. He just doesn't want you to interfere in their matters. Make no mistake - they do not trust you, and there's nothing you can do to make them.

Okay. Now that they've seen us - slow down a little more. That way, they know we're not trying to make any trouble. I'm not sure who that is -

the guy flagging us over. He might be one of the recruits.

He's going to tap on your window with his gun. Don't let it startle you - it's just a power move. He'll assume we're trying to get into the town based on the car we're in. Keep eye contact and tell him that we heard about their cause on the news and wanted to see how it had grown. Appeal to their ego. That's all many of them have left out here. The Crash of 2008 stole their pride, and the years since only made things worse for these folks.

We don't have too long. They'll continue to go about their business and not pay attention to us as long as they think we're just passing through.

And don't take any pictures.

We can get a little closer to the barricade now. I want you to see Ralph and his posse.

The guy in the sheepskin jacket who looks like a lumberjack - sitting in the driver's seat of that red pickup - that's Ray. And next to him - looks like Dickie is sitting shotgun. You can't see him that well - but he's what you imagine when someone is described as built like a brick shithouse. And he never goes anywhere without that mangy trucker hat. The guy in the blue ball cap heading towards the truck is Rayray. When he turns around, you'll see why all the women Charlene grew up with always tell her she caught herself "a real looker." He looks like one of those superheroes in the movies who is in hiding and lets his hair and beard grow out. See? What'd I tell you? I assume that piece of paper he just handed them is a supplies list of some sort. They're probably just about to head out.

You can see Bart and Ralph over near the tents. Ralph is the shaggy beanpole with the long beard. He doesn't usually wear cowboy hats. In fact, he never even owned a cowboy hat before the press started arriving. He went out and bought it one day to look "more authentic." That's a phrase he learned from Rayray. Bart is the adorable teddy bear in a ball cap like Rayray's, wearing a sheepskin jacket like Ray's. The ball cap he bought himself, the jacket is actually a hand-me-down from Ray. Ray kept growing after he hit Bart's size. Bart would be one of those dogs who always looks like a puppy.

Wally Combs is the one in the suit - with the TV anchor smile pasted over his depressed look - walking over to them. Wally's a reporter for the

Billings Gazette. Looks like they're about to make the news again.

Those porta potties are close enough that if we make like we're going over there to use them, we'll be able to eavesdrop on their conversation.

I really just have this one last thing I want you to hear before we leave:

"Mr. Elmore, I really think everyone in Montana should know about your efforts here -"

"Mm-hm."

"I just want to ask a few questions -"

"Mm-hm."

"What can I tell our readers about this cause you started."

"Cause?"

"The barricades? Not letting anyone in or out?"

"Not sure I'd call it a cause."

"And what would you call it?"

"A fucking shame. That's what they're bringing here into our home."

"And what do you hope to accomplish?"

"Gonna drive 'em out."

"All of them?"

"Every last one of them. We want them out

of Montana. The whole godamn shametown of
theirs."

PART ONE

TWO YEARS AGO

Chapter One

Here's how all of this began.

Rami and Brooke had never met before tonight. A year from now, they will be standing over a glass vase topped with toilet paper and Maxwell House coffee grounds attempting to make pour-over coffee because they don't yet own a coffee maker. As Rami pours boiling water over the grounds - trying not to scald Brooke as she holds the vase still - he'll laugh about the situation and ask her, "A year ago, would you have ever thought you'd be standing here doing this with me now?"

The answer, of course, is, "Fuck, no!"

That's because nothing is supposed to go wrong tonight. Quite literally, the point of tonight's meeting is to launch both of their respective careers into the stratosphere. For Brooke, the opportunity to write a piece that would open doors to job offers and book deals; for Rami, the chance to introduce himself to the world when the company he founded is on the precipice of one of the five largest IPOs in US history. For those of you who have spared yourself from the inner workings of America's venture capital hellscape: IPO is a fancy abbreviation for Initial Public Offering, which is a fancy way of saying the company is going public and the public can buy shares of stock. Ugh.

I hate to be the bearer of bad news, but things do not go well for either. If so, I wouldn't find these events so fascinating. Nor would they.

Nor would you.

Tonight's events were set into motion by a conversation had between the DoggyBag Board of Directors and the company's spindly, bespectacled COO, Darrell Weems.

Darrell was Rami's first prominent investor and the first to see the potential in what Rami was building. Darrell understood what DoggyBag could become, which is often different than what the founder initially built. But American Business plays by its own rules, and Darrell's money came at a cost to Rami that he didn't find too high when signing the papers. Looking back at it in a year, Rami will see this whole dance as a period of absurdity in his life.

But at that time, Rami trusted Darrell wholeheartedly and took his guidance as gospel. And Darrell and the Board were worried that Rami's reclusivity might prevent the IPO from reaching the price they believed it could.

"Investors are investing in the CEO's vision more than the company's track record," Gene Alredd, Treasurer of the Board, said at one point during this conversation. Rebecca Woolfram, Vice President of the Board, quickly interjected, "And the CEO's vision is even more critical for a startup that's barely old enough to have a track record! Darrell, you must convince him to do an interview."

And that was how all of this began.

Well, I suppose the founding of DoggyBag is where all of this really begins.

Which technically begins with Hanibal Mahmoud, Rami's father, immigrating his wife Yasmin and their newborn son from Egypt to a splat of land in Northern California that would one day come to be called Silicon Valley.

His first job, coding an application for a wild new piece of tech on the market: the personal computer, sealed Rami's fate the moment Hanibal typed his first line of code. His imagination raced while he sat as a young child watching his father compose symphonies in programming languages he would master before even entering kinder-garten.

In 1991, Hanibal took a job in Chicago and moved his family from the West Coast. The lib-eralness of Silicon Valley made Hanibal uncom-fortable. He didn't want his son raised in that environment, certainly not as he entered his teen-age years. He feared Rami was too impressionable to grow up on the West Coast and still adhere to their faith. Rami's sensitivity as a child always irked Hanibal - he made comment to Yasmin many times that she didn't do enough to discour-age his behavior. When Rami cried, she held him. When he was scared, she protected him. Rami had the "better life" that Hanibal always dreamed of - but it didn't appear to be helping his son become a man. Staying in California seemed like it would only exacerbate (what he saw as) the problem.

Rami never developed a social life in High School. "Friends" were really just study partners. And when he went to the University of Chicago, nothing changed. He never drank, never did any drugs, never had sex. Instead, he studied, volunteered at the closest mosque - an unspoken, though non-negotiable expectation of Hanibal's - and occasionally attended events held by the Muslim student group on campus.

He did want all of the things he denied himself. He could have had them. More of his fellow students had a crush on him than he would ever guess. There weren't a lot of tall, dark, curly-haired guys on campus with naturally smoky eyes. He was striking to look at, even if a bit underweight. A girl in one of his classes, Angela, made it well known to him in various ways - often graphic - that she would sleep with him if he wanted to. He didn't want to. But he needed to. At least, it felt like he needed to. But he couldn't bring himself to pursue.

Shortly after he graduated college, something new rocked the industry: Apple launched a store within iTunes where independent developers could develop and sell apps to iPhone owners.

Apps.

When he told his parents about his plan to try his hand at the app game, their poor reaction actually flummoxed him. Well, his dad's poor reaction. His whole life - without fail - his mom sided with his father, even when Rami knew she disagreed. Their "secret agreement," Rami described it to… himself. (I mean… Who else could he describe it to other than his parents - which would make for a very awkward conversation?)t

It truly baffled Hanibal that Rami didn't want to apply to "good jobs" at IBM or Microsoft. Rami tried to make him understand: laptops no longer represented the future of portable computing. Phones were the new future. Needless to say, his efforts to convince Hanibal accomplished exactly nothing.

But for the first time in his life, he didn't do what his father wanted. He did what he wanted.

And it felt strange. Good, but strange. Like unlocking some suppressed part of himself.

He moved out of his parents' house and found an apartment. He took a consulting job to pay the bills but spent every other waking hour developing apps. You haven't heard of any of his first apps. They, like most apps, simply didn't take off. Rami remained undeterred, though.

Until one day, the idea for DoggyBag struck him, and the rest, as they say, is history.

Well, not all of the rest.

But! All you need to know right now is that Rami made a shit ton of money, drew exponentially more attention than he wanted, and *finally* made his father proud.

Chapter Two

I'm not saying that destiny is responsible for these events as they happened. This isn't a purposeful meditation on fate. The events that happened happened as they happened the same way that many pivotal moments in our lives happen: because of some dumb mistake.

It was a long day for Brooke. She woke up at 4 AM that morning to get downtown in time to cover the Black Lives Matter boycott. The boycott started at 7 AM, and she wanted to be there before the first people began to arrive. And she didn't want to look like she had just rolled out of bed. She's always known she doesn't meet the standards of the typical American version of beauty. She's not tall - 5' 8" on a good day, is what she told her new doctor recently. Her hair is black, not blonde, and catastrophically curly on most days, not wavy or straight. She takes after her dad, so she spent a childhood of her mother reminding her that American girls are skinnier. So she puts a good deal of effort into her appearance, and that meant a 4 AM wake-up call. I guess the good news for her is that this is her last early wake-up call for work. She will enjoy that. She won't enjoy the reason the Tribune doesn't send her on early morning stories after today.

Still standing in the middle of Michigan Avenue, just before 6 PM, she received the call from her editor: What was she doing tonight? Rami from DoggyBag agreed to an interview - in fact, his first interview ever - and he wants her to write it. The jolt of adrenaline that flooded her system renewed her in a way she never previously experienced. It felt righteous. And in the heat of the moment, she blurted out, "Where and when should I meet him?"

The meeting would take place over dinner. Her editor texted her the details. And then, just before she put her phone in her bag, he texted her one last instruction: He agreed to let you live tweet the evening.

This was the ideal situation. She would be able to build anticipation for the full article by dropping exciting tidbits as the interview takes place. Just enough to whet her followers' appetites while leaving the juiciest stuff for the big story.

Brooke is what is now commonly known as "aAn "Influencer." She personally despises that designation and particularly loathes when her family uses it. Nevertheless, her father loves introducing her to people - even those who already know her - as "Brooke De los Arcos, Ch'cago Influencér!"

Admittedly, she does always crack a smile hearing how it sounds with her dad's unique Chicago-meets-Mexico dialect. "Mexicago," she called it.

But how could her family not be proud of her accomplishments?

Growing up in Chicago, the daughter of two undocumented immigrants, she watched too many like her get stuck in jobs only slightly better than their parents. Her dad worked in an auto body shop up in Edgewater, and her mom worked in a panaderia under the Red Line tracks near the Sheridan stop. Neither sShe nor her parents wanted the same for her.

After graduating at the top of her high school class, she opted to attend Truman College in Chicago rather than a "more prestigious" school like many of her classmates. She knew she wanted to go into journalism - and Medill sat just a few stops away - and a transfer to the Purple Line - on the CTA. But she knew - unlike many of her classmates - that it was doubtful her parents would ever afford retirement, and she found the idea of sinking the family into student loan debt unthinkable. So she opted to complete her undergraduate studies in three years and then attend Medill as a graduate student.

During her time at Medill, her knack for financial journalism surprised her. Her upbringing came with complete awareness of home finances, watching her parents negotiate bills through their paycheck-to-paycheck life. This informed her own approach to money management, but it had not occurred to her that perhaps there were others out there that could benefit from learning how she does it.

Fortunately, it did occur to her after a serendipitous evening with her roommate's sister.

Her roommate Anita had sublet her room to

Marissa while she took a semester abroad. One night, Marissa was up late trying to finish editing a short film she'd shot while in Chicago - she wanted to get it done before Anita returned and she had to move back to Iowa.

Brooke came home late that night and planned on going straight to bed, but Marissa caught her as she opened the front door and asked if she would watch the film. Brooke was astonished by what Marissa had made. Marissa showed her the different gadgets she used to film her short using her iPhone camera. As a trade-off, Brooke showed Marissa how she could install an app on her phone that automatically rounded up every purchase on her debit card and deposited the change into an investment account.

"Are you fucking kidding me?" Marissa said, gawking at the phone.

"No?" Brooke asked warily.

"I thought that would be hard!" Marissa said with a smile.

And there it was: the inspiration for the project that would make Brooke famous.

When she saw how easy it was to get Marissa to start investing, even if just a little bit at a time, it occurred to her that much of her generation had not begun saving up for retirement and probably hadn't even started saving up to buy their next computer, and she thought the barrier they imagined between them and their ability to invest was probably much smaller than they feared.

Most people don't understand finances. Only a fraction of the public reconciles and balances their accounts at the end of each month. It's a foreign language.

What if she made it easy to digest by showing them what she was doing? Better yet: what if she showed them what they were doing?

The day after she graduated, she created a blog, YouTube channel, and social media accounts where she would provide financial advice for Millennials and Gen Z. The first months only brought in a few viewers and followers - nothing to brag about, and a source of concern she may be wasting her time. Things changed, though, when WGN featured one of her clips on their morning show. Suddenly, she was receiving offers to write articles for other publications and appear as a special guest on live TikToks.

But the real prize - a full-time job as a

professional journalist at a respected publication - eventually came knocking: a call from the Finance Editor at the Chicago Tribune. They wanted to give her her own column. They wanted her to continue making videos - but specifically to be hosted on their site. They would drive traffic to her social media channels (rebranded under the Trib, of course.) They would launch her with a billboard campaign and plaster the sides of CTA buses with her image. She represented the future of the Tribune. She was what they had been waiting for.

And so she signed with them. WGN gave her a weekly segment. Her readership and viewership grew exponentially. The Tonight Show had her on as a guest. SNL even wrote a sketch about her.

Her dreams had come true.

Here's where the bomb that will rip their two lives apart begins to be constructed, bit by bit, sip by sip.

The choice of restaurant instantly set the stage.

Alinea.

One of the "it" restaurants not only in Chicago but the world.

His first move is undoubtedly to make an impression, she thought to herself when she first read the details. And thus, her first tweet, standing on the sidewalk outside the restaurant: A photo of Alinea with the caption, There's a first time for everything.

It was her first time at Alinea. She never expected to dine here on her own dollar in a million years. A journalist's salary would never cover the tab, so her only hope was a situation like this.

Her phone vibrated. "I'm inside sitting near the bar. Take your time. No rush" read Rami's text.

No rush, she thought to herself. What does that mean? Is he just being polite? She expected him to be in a hurry to run off to whatever more critical meeting came next on his agenda. No rush, she said to herself again. There is something here - her instinct for digging to the truth piqued.

As she entered the restaurant, she said it to herself again: No rush.

She recognized him immediately, sitting alone and nervously playing with his mustache. The media plastered his face all over the internet with each of DoggyBag's milestone achievements. Of course, she saw no reason why he would know her from any other stranger off the street. Why would he? But as she started towards the table, he looked up and waved. "Brooke! It's nice to meet you in person."

Nice to meet me in person, she thought. "Is it?" she said with an embarrassed laugh. This seemed to catch him by surprise. He became awkward and unsure and, in doing so, became just a little more charming.

"I'm sorry, is that weird to say?" he asked, demurring even more.

"No! I'm sorry. I'm sorry. That's - I don't know..." She started laughing awkwardly and suddenly realized that she might be unable to stop. She had the church giggles.

And then she noticed: so did he.

She finally settled in at the table after a bizarre dance of giggles and taking off her coat and trying to hang it over the back of her chair and him trying to get out of his chair to help her when someone materialized behind her, pulled out her chair, grabbed her coat, and just as suddenly disappeared, leaving no wake, like an Olympic diver.

"Cheers," he offered, hoisting his wine glass to her and spilling on the candle between them.

Through the smoke of the snuffed-out center-piece, she clinked her glass against his.

And the two both took a healthy, long sip of their first glass.

The awkwardness passed for a moment and then returned with a vengeance.

Now what, they both thought.

"I'm sorry, this is my first interview," Rami said, hoping to break the tension. "I'm not entirely sure..." He stopped, not entirely sure what he wanted to say.

"Well, you're the most... 'famous' interviewee of my career," she offered.

At this, he swallowed and found that there were no words. Until finally, he managed, "I'm not famous." Which he knew was a lie. But it wasn't entirely false either. Rami the CEO of DoggyBag, may be famous, but Rami the human being remained a mystery.

"Well, don't let me quote you on that, or no one will want to read my article," she half-joked.

"Oh, that was absolutely off the record," he said with a smile.

She didn't know what to make of how at ease he put her. Rami somehow comforted her and felt familiar even though they only met moments ago. She couldn't place it. It almost felt like deja vu. Like they were only friends meeting to catch up after not seeing each other for several years.

More sweet nerd from high school than Elon Musk, @ramimahmoud's humility is a refreshing first impression, Brooke tweeted.

Rami's phone pinged. They both smiled, separately, at the moment. "I'll read that one later," he joked, pulling out his phone and silencing it.•

"So you run your own Twitter account?"

"Mine, yes. DoggyBag's, no.

"Is it important to you that you speak for yourself?" she inquired.

"Oh, wow. Okay. Just jumping in, are we?"

She smiled and put down her phone but said nothing - keeping the following reply in his court.

"I suppose. I'm a fairly private person."

"He says without divulging absolutely anything," she teased with a rye wry smile.

"Fair."

"Tell me one thing about you that no one knows," she challenged.

"I play piano," he said without hesitation.

He came with that one in the chamber, she thought.

"A musician?"

"Ah. No. Not a musician. I stopped playing seriously in high school."

"Can you still play?"

He smiled. He knew what she would ask next as soon as he replied in the affirmative.

"I've still got some Ben Folds in my back pocket."

Little known fact: Rami's a secret Ben Foldsaphile. Maybe we'll get a mini recital later if I can find a piano…

At the very moment of that tweet, you would be forgiven for not seeing how it brought the explosive that awaited them both one step closer to completion. The seemingly insignificant microevents of our lives often have the most impact.

In some alternate reality where things went very differently: Brooke never sent that tweet and Rami didn't joke around about his piano at home, so she never proposed a recital. Since he does not offer up the opportunity - even in the tiniest of ways - for the interview to continue beyond dinner, Brooke has no reason to end up at his home. And both continue their lives per their original plans.

Wouldn't that be nice for them? But: then that would be where their story ends. And you'd have no reason to ever care about Rami and Brooke. And I'd have no one to tell this story to. For what reason would there be to tell their story? What story would there be to tell?

This, as we both know, is not their current predicament. Their current predicament is that everything is going exactly as they are supposed to in this reality.

Rami was in the process of self-maneuvering himself into a corner and, it seemed, had no choice but to make good on the offer when it occurred to him that he wasn't entirely in control. He was…

He was drunk.

Not drunk-drunk. But definitely intoxicated.

He rarely, if ever, drank. He had what you might call a low tolerance. And he'd assumed wine would not hit him too hard or fast.

Wrong, Rami, he thought to himself.

Well, he would just stop where he was at and switch to water.

"We'll take two more," Brooke said to the server, motioning to the two wine glasses.

So much for that idea, Rami thought.

I won't bore you with the full details of their dinner. It lasted ninety minutes, and Rami shared more than he meant to - and with every more interesting tweet, Brooke took another sip of wine and inched them closer to destruction.

At this point, the actual explosive has been thoroughly engineered, and all that remains is the fuse.

Rami would provide that piece.

As they left the restaurant, Brooke saw Rami pull out his phone to call a Lyft.

"Didn't you promise me a private piano concert?" Brooke half-teased, hoping that he would oblige.

Rami thought about it for a second. This could be a dangerous extension of their interview, especially as the last couple of glasses of wine started to hit. But he liked being uninhibited, even for just one night. And for some reason, he felt unusually comfortable talking with Brooke.

Most people made him feel like an alien,

trying to make conversation in a foreign language. That, however, is not who Brooke is. She makes him comfortable. More surprising: she makes him comfortable being himself. That's new. And, in its own way, as intoxicating as anything they consumed that night.

Tapping on the shortcut for his home, Rami called a Lyft. "Let's do it."

And with that, they unknowingly, but perfectly, installed the fuse in their weapon of self-destruction.

Arriving at his condo overlooking Millennium Park, Brooke is breath-taken by the view. This is what he wakes up to, she thought.

"I don't really know what any of this is," he said from behind her. She turned to see him standing at an open wine cabinet, fifty bottles of what she imagined were very expensive wines staring him in the face.

"You don't know what wine you own?" she laughed.

"It was for a photo shoot for some promo thing... The photographer decided something sophisticated needed to compliment the background.

She said that my walls were too bare." He laughed at this. Looking around, both took stock of the absolute absence of anything on his bare, white walls.

Running her fingers over the bottles, she would stop now and then to pull one out and look at the label.

"Oh! This is a nice shiraz," she said a little too loud.

"You a wine connoisseur?" he asked with a hint of worry.

"No. But I am a wine label connoisseur." She held the bottle out for him to see. "Who can say no to a bunch of goats leaping around a mountainside?"

After a few seconds of silence, she went to her purse and started rummaging around. "I assume you don't have a wine opener," she stated dryly.

He didn't.

"It's okay. I always keep one on me," she said, pulling a small contraption out of her bag.

As she wrestled the cork out of the bottle, she heard the tinkling of piano keys coming from the other room.

When she turned the corner, Rami sat at an

old, beaten upright piano with two wine glasses sitting on top.

"What's your request?"

"Oh, man. That's tough. I have to admit; I'm also a big Ben Folds fan. There're so many to choose from."

"Okay," he said, turning to her, one hand gripping the top of the piano, the other lightly resting on the keyboard, "What's your favorite?" he asked as she snapped a quick photo.

Most Eligible Bachelor? she tweeted as the caption.

The fuse was lit.

As he began playing, she walked to the floor-to-ceiling windows that looked out over Lake Michigan at night, the city lights reflecting at her. Taking a sip from her glass, she heard him start to sing. He sounded great. Who would have ever suspected?

And then it popped into her head. The incendiary marriage of burning fuse and combustible material was about to be consummated.

She tapped off one final tweet just seconds before her phone died: Multimillion-dollar sunrise views are the ultimate date rape drug.

Then the Apple logo, hovering against a black void, overcame her screen before blinking out of existence. Snuffed out, it would seem, from the blowback of the explosion that had just ripped through their lives, unbeknownst to either of them.

They would continue talking and drinking and, to their surprise, develop a friendship of sorts. At the very least, they would meet up one more time, but as a social occasion.

Or so they thought. With Rami's phone silenced and plugged in on his bedside table and Brooke's dead in her purse, neither was receiving the onslaught of panicked texts, calls, and emails.

When Brooke left, she took public transportation home. And when she plugged in her phone after arriving home, she was too tired - and beginning to feel hungover - to notice that the other end of the cord wasn't plugged into an electrical outlet.

It would be another six or so hours before either would see the news.

It would be devastating.

It would be the end of Rami's professional career.

It would be the beginning of the end of Brooke's.

But that's not what this story is about. So let's get through this part quickly, shall we?

Chapter Three

It was bad.

Worse than they were prepared for. Though how could anyone at DoggyBag have been ready for this situation?

It happened in an instant. So fast that Rami barely knew the time of day at any moment - it seemed like everything was happening at once.

It was.

The tweet, as you have likely assumed, had gone viral.

Brooke slept while most of this occurred. She would soon regret not plugging in her phone as soon as she got home. Two full hours passed after Rami announced his departure before she learned what machine she had set into motion with a mere twelve words.

A phone call woke Rami unceremoniously before he saw the news. On the other end, Darrell Weems, Current COO - and soon-to-be Co-CEO - blathered at full volume and a frantic pace, in apocalyptic terms. In his hungover capacity, Rami tried to piece together Darrell's ranting. But upon grabbing his glasses from the foot of the bed - where they lay because he passed out entirely clothed - he saw the badge on his Twitter app icon blared a 99+ in bright red.

His mind was not so hung over that he couldn't quickly connect the dots between Darrell's hyperventilating, the barrage of Twitter notifications and Brooke's tweeting the night before.

He opened the Twitter app but trying to scroll through the notifications overwhelmed him. The terms thrown around - rapist, predator, aggressor - were so shocking that his mind wouldn't allow him to compute why these adjectives appeared before his name. Over and over again.

"We needed you in the office *hours ago!*" Darrell shouted after finally assembling his thoughts.

The call ended. Rami continued holding the phone to his ear as he tried to piece together everything happening at that moment.

He didn't have time for that. He just needed to get to the office.

After a solid 20 or 30 seconds of searching for his phone, he finally remembered that his other hand was in possession of the device. "Hey, Siri, get me to the office."

"I didn't quite get that. Can you please repeat the request?" Siri seemed to scream in his ear.

"No, stop!" he whispered as loudly as he could before finally pulling up the Lyft app himself and requesting a ride.

Four minutes. That was how much time he had to get dressed and out the door.

But first, he needed to vomit.

❖

Stepping out of the elevator, nervously straightening and loosening and tightening his tie, Rami concluded - correctly, mind you - how this would all play out and arrive at its logical finale.

There were more people at the office than he'd expected. For a Saturday, the kitchen area was packed more than usual.

Gawkers, Rami thought to himself. They've never seen an execution before.

As he neared the conference room, Rami

wondered, Is there any point in fighting this? He stopped outside the room and took a deep breath.

"I didn't do it!" Rami blurted out as he slid open the conference room door. "I didn't do anything!"

"Of course you didn't," Darrell assured him as he slid in on his right side and guided him to a chair. "But right now, your primary goal is to ensure that your employees keep their jobs."

Keep their jobs, Rami thought to himself.

"We are on the cusp of a historic IPO," Darrell continued.

"We just need to explain..." Rami began before Sheila Mahal, the new CFO, cut him off.

"Rami. Listen. There are over 12,000 people whose livelihoods will be dramatically impacted by this IPO. For better or worse. There are shareholders - investors who believed in you early on - who are looking at a massive loss if it flounders," Sheila impressed upon him.

After a few seconds of letting this sink in - the enormity of what was at stake, all because of a string of letters and spaces shot into cyberspace - he asked with a break in his voice, "What do we do?"

"That's what we're working on..." Sheila began

again but was interrupted by the nervous break-down that Rami started having as she was speak-ing.

The room looked at each other, hoping some-one would know how to handle this moment of terrible discomfort, until finally Darrell pulled out his phone and told Rami, "Look, let me call you a ride home - you need to…"

"I need to call Brooke!" Rami shouted, fumbling for his phone.

"No, no - don't call anyone, that's the last thing…" Darrell said, trying to talk Rami down.

"She can explain!" Rami said, rushing out of the conference room.

Darrell caught Rami at the elevator and grabbed his phone out of his hand.

"Rami. Every single little thing that is said or done over the next 24 hours will determine how you get out of this. Do not do anything stupid." Rami nodded. Darrell handed him his phone and then turned back to his own, completing the Uber request. "Go home, don't go online, and wait for my call. Just lay low. Okay?" Rami didn't answer. "Okay?" Rami nodded half-heartedly as the eleva-tor arrived.

"Going down," the elevator heckled him.

Rami made... thirteen calls to Brooke on his ride home. Though she received none of them due to her full voicemail box, so he couldn't leave a message.

Brooke was just waking up during his eleventh attempt. On his twelfth call, she realized her phone hadn't actually been plugged in overnight and was dead to the world. It took another four minutes after his final call before she finally plugged it in on her bathroom counter and started the shower.

While shampooing her hair, the phone came to life with a cacophony of notifications. After the notifications continued past the point she could keep count, she froze for a second. What the fuck is going on?! she thought.

The notifications still pealing, the phone starting to ring is what caused her to open her eyes suddenly and send shards of lather streaming in. Rushing to rinse the burning sensation out while flailing for a towel, she tripped over the lip of the bathtub and went sprawling on the floor, a spider-web of cracks spraying across her phone screen and blotting out any ability to read.

But it continued to ring. She couldn't read the caller ID but answered anyhow out of urgency. "Hello?!" she shouted over the running shower.

"Is this Brooke De los Arcos?"

"Speaking?" Brooke confirmed with hesitation.

"This is Mark Weiner from the Wall Street Journal…"

Brooke hung up.

"What the fuck?!" she said out loud to herself.

She looked at her phone and tried to dial her editor. But she couldn't read anything or type to search for anyone.

Her laptop. How the fuck had she forgotten about that?!

Leaving a trail of small puddles behind her, she ran to the bedroom and yanked her laptop out of its sleeve. She opened her email… and watched as a stream of hundreds of emails flowed into her inbox.

Her slack app started ringing.

It was her editor.

"I'm sorry, I just got out of the shower…." Brooke shouted over the running water.

"Brooke…"

"… and my phone had died…" she continued.

"Brooke, I need…."

"…and my screen is cracked, so I can't -"

"Brooke!" She snapped out of her spiral. "We need to talk about how we're handling this situation."

Brooke froze. After a second, her muscles kicked back in, and she quickly ran back to the bathroom to shut the water off. "What situation?" she accidentally asked out loud.

"With Rami."

"What about Rami?" Brooke asked, her imagination running wild. Was he hurt? Had he died? Abducted? But the truth would never cross her mind.

"The Tweet, Brooke. Your last Tweet."

She couldn't remember her last tweet. But once her editor began to fill her in on the last few hours' happenings, every character of the text started to sear into her memory. What had she been thinking?! Her mind went blank of what to say or do. Time abandoned her and left her floating untethered from the rest of the world moving around her.

"Are you alright? Did he do anything?" her editor inquired with some uncharacteristic formality.

"Do anything? Absolutely not!" Brooke spoke the last two words clearly and intentionally to eliminate any misunderstanding. "It was... a stupid..." As she tried to explain, she realized she had no reasonable excuse. She stopped. She suddenly needed to sit down.

"Brooke?"

Her legs didn't want to stand anymore. Without warning, she sat on the bathroom's tile floor. She placed the phone on the toilet seat and put her head in her hands. "It was a joke," she said with dissipating energy. "I was joking."

As she sat there, dazed, she listened to her editor rattle off what would happen from here, but she absorbed little and retained none of it. The words weren't in any language she spoke. Just some distant mumblespeak she'd never heard. Until the words, "...Twitter account has been deleted." And then lightning struck, and she was standing again.

"I just need to explain!" She rushed back into the bedroom, grabbing her laptop.

"Didn't you hear -" her editor attempted.

"I can edit the Tweet and comment -"

"That's what I'm saying, Brooke. Your company Twitter account is gone. Deleted."

She froze in her tracks. Her mind was a blur of racing thoughts and emotions. She tried to parse together a reasonable response but only came up with, "Why?" The sound of her editor sighing followed.

"We are trying to get through this without making any more waves. We can't -"

"But if I can -" Brooke interrupted before her editor spoke over her with uncharacteristic force.

"We cannot be responsible for a failed Doggy-Bag IPO. This wasn't supposed to be investigative journalism. It wasn't even supposed to be a story. It was supposed to be a simple profile of a tech entrepreneur."

"And I get that -" Brooke interjected.

"Brooke, please!"

Brooke stopped. She felt like a child being scolded.

"We got this opportunity because our parent company is a major investor in Doggy Bag."

Brooke hadn't known this.

"And if any of us are going to keep our jobs after this fucking debacle, it's because the IPO happens without a hitch as if none of this ever happened. Okay?"

Brooke made some barely-audible noise in acknowledgment.

"You are not to take any interviews. Don't answer any calls from numbers you don't recognize. For at least the next few days, only leave your home if absolutely necessary. And if you do, do not speak to anyone. We are printing a retraction and apology tomorrow morning, and hopefully, that will make this all blow over, and we can all move on."

Brooke couldn't tell if he expected a response.

"And under no circumstances are you to contact or interact with Rami. Understood?"

Rami. In her waking whirlwind, she never even stopped to think about what this must be doing to him. He was the one person she wanted to speak with right now.

"Brooke?"

"Yes."

A few seconds of silence. Her editor tried to prepare for the next part of the conversation. She could tell. She could hear that signature deep inhale and held breath she had experienced countless times as she waited for an answer to whatever question she had asked. Then came the exhale and familiar start to a perfectly crafted response:

"Look, I always have your back," her editor began, "and I'm hoping this does not take us down a path where our mutual separation is necessary."

A pause to see if she had any reaction.

"And we feel that the best way to make that a likely outcome is to put you on paid leave for a few weeks."

Brooke took this in and turned it over in her mind. "Am I being fired?" she asked with as much composure as she could muster.

"Absolutely not. That is not what I'm saying. But we always want to prepare for the worst-case scenario. Right?" Brooke's silence was affirmation enough. "I'll call you later when I have more updates."

"Thank you," was all Brooke could think to say. And then her editor ended the call.

As with all the best-laid plans, things did not go according to plan.

The retraction and statement had minimal impact on public perception. However, that can be mainly attributed to the left-wing and right-wing arms of the media pouncing on the opportunity to roast the kind of Silicon Valley darling they love to loathe.

It started when a conservative blogger did the math and realized that due to the happenstance of shared ownership, the Tribune had an incentive to make DoggyBag's problems disappear. Did they really want their piggy bank to go broke?

While the right screamed about the media elite's nefarious backroom dealings and rampant corruption, the left enjoyed a shouting match about the toxic workplace Rami's actions created and how the lessons of #metoo still needed to be learned by America's privileged, male corporate leaders.

Honestly, I found it exhausting. I watched and read and listened to all of it so that you don't need to. And believe me - I'm saving you from a migraine-a-thon. I think both sides are mostly comprised of asshat idiots who prefer masturbating to recordings of their own blathering than listening to a damn thing the constituents of their respective domains have to say regarding the quality of their own lives. And don't give me that bullshit about "how they brought it on themselves by buying and voting for those in power." You know why that's bullshit? Because most people don't have the privilege of choice. Or they get stuck with a choice between a hemorrhoidal dingbat and a flagellating anal wart.

It didn't take long for the Board to decide that there was no getting around it: Rami had to go. While the Tribune did what it could to clear up the misunderstanding, it was already out of anyone's control. The narrative being told by the clickbait-hungry media was not pretty. And they could not go into the IPO with any baggage like this.

I'm only going to go over the bullet points here because I like Rami and hate to recount every painful detail.

The Board chose Darrell to deliver the news. Rami sat there silently and unmoving the entire time Darrell spoke. At the end of Darrell's outlining of what would happen next, he nodded and went to his bedroom, letting Darrell see himself out.

Rami didn't even read his resignation letter or statement. He learned what he "said" weeks later when he finally got back on the internet, and his curiosity took hold.

His "voluntary" resignation came with a package worth more than eight hundred million.

And really couldn't give fewer fucks.

As he heard the door close behind Darrell, he closed his eyes and rolled over.

And didn't leave his bedroom for a week.

When Brooke saw the news of Rami's resignation, she stopped in her tracks. Standing in the middle of Wells St, she stared at her phone until a car horn scared her back into the world.

Days after Rami's resignation became official, the Tribune reinstated Brooke full-time. Though, her assignments would cover subjects far less likely to create any sort of conflagration.

But as badly as she wanted to keep her job, the news could not pull her out of the self-loathing haze she was living in now. She smiled to try to make herself happy. But it didn't have the intended effect. It just made her feel worse.

Because of her fuckup, Rami lost the company he founded while she got to keep her job.

Karma is coming for me, she thought to herself.

And not incorrectly.

Chapter Four

So - to be completely transparent with you - what followed the immediate aftermath of Rami's imploded life is too depressing to recount here for you. To give you an idea of how well Rami handled things: it was months, actually, before he decided to start to rejoin the living world. About nine months, to be exact. Plus another 30 days or so.

I don't want to overwhelm you with a downright morbid, nearly 10-month-long tale of woe. Which this isn't. Oh, it will indeed have its fair share of morbidity and woe, but not that much.

So we'll skip to the day Rami turned on his computer.

And immediately learned that he had to upgrade to the latest operating system.

Okay, so it wasn't a great first sign about how

much the universe wanted him to return to a life ruled by the laws of gravity and currency. Still, he forged ahead and decided to make coffee for the first time in several months - about nine months, plus another 30 days or so, to be approximately exact - while the slab of cold metal and glass spent the next 20 minutes learning how to be a better computer.

When the familiar megachordal chime of his laptop finally came to life, he felt it inside his chest. Like he, too, was being booted back up.

I haven't listened to music in forever, he thought to himself.

He meandered over to where he kept his record collection and took a sip of his coffee. I've missed this, he thought. Picking up Janelle Monae's The ArchAndroid, he carefully removed it from its sleeve and admired it. A record is a thing of beauty. It is music manifested in physical form. Tapes and CDs and digital tracks don't proudly wear the melodies you are about to enjoy on their surfaces. They try to hide it beneath their sleek exteriors, trying to take center stage from the tunes.

He turned up the volume and went back to his laptop.

His icon stared at him. He logged in. And the apps he had instructed the computer to start automatically began to pop up, window by window, at an alarming rate. For a moment, he felt overwhelmed and almost slammed it shut. But he had done that plenty. He just needed to rip off the bandaid.

An avalanche of emails flooded into his inbox. His first instinct urged him to select and delete all of them without looking. But that would be unreasonably reactionary and, again, just giving in to avoidance. He clicked on his priority inbox. This one only showed emails from people in his contacts. And since he didn't have a lot of friends and kept his work contacts separate from his personal contacts, he didn't have a ton of emails to slog through.

A lot of condolences, or whatever you say to someone who lost their life's work in one fell swoop due to no error of their own. A few interview offers from friends who went into journalism or considered themselves well-respected bloggers/vloggers/podcasters/social influencers.

Though one email did catch his attention. It was from his DoggyBag co-founder, Rajesh.

He and Raj met in college the second semester of their first year and got an apartment together the summer before junior year. Both considered themselves - and were considered by others - introverts but felt like extroverts in the company of each other.

He hadn't spoken to Raj in years.

Theirs was the typical, shitty start-up story about best-friend-founders who are driven apart by early investors who want to seat their own people in the leadership roles currently being held by the most clever kids who started the whole thing but were fooling themselves if they thought they had any idea how actually to run a company. The easiest way to accomplish this transition is to make the CEO the youthful face of the company while - in the background - moving out the founding staff and bringing in the people with shareholder interests top of mind. And that is precisely what Darrell Weems did.

Very swiftly, Darrell brought in investors and diluted Raj's controlling interest in the company through all kinds of shady, multi-reaem documents and legal maneuvers. Rami saw it happening but kept telling himself that it was better for one of them to remain in a top leadership position so that what they built together doesn't die, and at least Raj's shares will increase in value, and he'll be set for life. That's what he told himself. He never said that to Raj. He rarely spoke to Raj. Not because he was avoiding him or didn't want to - but Darrell managed Rami's schedule to ensure that there were as few opportunities as possible for the two of them to speak. He didn't need Raj appealing to Rami's feelings for him.

Darrell needed to cut this thing off, though. It was taking up too much of his time to manage. So he made his move.

The Board voted to terminate Raj as COO and install Darrell as Interim-COO. Of course, interim was just a word put in front of the letters COO to make it look like he wasn't going to be taking over more and more control of the company on behalf of the Board. He was just a friendly investor, happy to step in and offer a helping hand while the company transitioned through a challenging time.

When Darrell gave him the news - which he had anticipated for a long time but lived in denial of its likelihood - Rami asked to tell Raj.

And telling Raj was the last thing that he ever

said to Raj. And "fuck you" was the last thing Raj ever said to Rami.

Until this email.

Rami wasn't sure if he wanted to open this one either. What could Raj possibly say to him that he wanted to hear? Was this going to be his long-awaited "told you so"? When they argued that last time they spoke, Raj said that if they were willing to do this to him, they'd be willing to do it to Rami whenever it would most benefit the shareholders. And here we were.

Well, whatever he has to say, it can't pull me down any further than I am already, Rami thought to himself. And then opened the email.

Hi Rami,

I'm sure you weren't expecting to hear from me. I wasn't really sure if I was going to reach out. But I know you have no one else who knows you like I do.

Look, I think I know what's going on right now. I empathize with your situation; you know I do. But it's time to move on. You can stop hiding from it and face reality. You can stop living your life for others. This is the chance we used to talk about. I think you know that. I think knowing that is why you're hiding.

So I'm offering a friendly hand to help you do it. My husband works at Reddit, and you are one of the most requested guests for Ask Me Anything. If you are interested, reply back, and I'll put you in touch.

I hope things get better for you.

- Raj

Rami sat, stunned. He had not expected that at all. And before he could second guess anything, he quickly hit reply and responded.

Thank you, Raj. I'd like to do the AMA.

- Mi

And then he hit send, his heart racing and breath held. He quickly stood up and walked away from the computer. He couldn't be near it during the 20 seconds grace period when it allowed him to recall the message before it was officially sent.

His heart stopped with a thought. Had he?

He practically killed himself getting back to the laptop and began rapidly clicking the Sent box to open it. He opened the email he'd just sent to Raj.

- Mi

And sure enough, he had. He suddenly felt sad and cold all over.

No one had called him "Mi" since Raj greeted him the last night they spoke.

Correction. No one called him "Mi" except Raj.

He made his way back into the bedroom and lay down. It wasn't until he noticed his pillow was damp that he realized he'd been crying. And then, in an instant, all of it - the whole last ten months, the dismissal of Raj, the death of his dreams - came rushing up and out of him as he wailed until he was hoarse.

The idea that made him a multimillionaire came to him after his neighbor's restaurant closed.

After they graduated from the University of Chicago, Rami and Raj decided to stay roommates but move to the more scenic neighborhood of Lincoln Square. Rami found them an austere but welcoming apartment above a small Italian restaurant not too far from the Rockwell stop on the Brown Line. The restaurant's kitchen was actually in the front of the restaurant, and each night, the owner and chef, Emilio, would wink at Rami whenever he came home in the evening. It wasn't long before he and Raj were regulars, stopping by for a drink - non-alcoholic, of course, as Rami and Raj were still abstaining from alcohol. Raj's husband would eventually break him of this "terrible habit," as he called it. You already know how much of a lightweight Rami is when it comes to the intoxicating effects of fermentation.

One night, when he and Raj were walking home from the train, Rami noticed from a distance that the restaurant's sign wasn't lit. It was Friday; the restaurant would be open unless something went wrong. As he neared, he saw Emilio cleaning in the dark, wearing a headlamp. He knocked on the window, and a hang-faced Emilio opened the door a long moment later. When Rami inquired about the night off, Emilio sat and let out a long sigh.

The electricity had been shut off. He couldn't keep up with all the bills - and his options were buying meat and produce or paying ComEd. He had hoped that business would pick up and he could start paying down his electric bill. But every week, he lost more money.

Rami's problem-solving brain heard this, and with it came that familiar tug. There was something here. Something he felt like he could fix.

Before his consulting instincts fully kicked in, Raj was suddenly asking Emilio if he could see his financials and ask him some questions.

In that moment, something zipped through Rami's being. A jolt that got his heart racing. Through all of their late-night conversations and lengthy debates, he'd often felt like the two of them were on the same wavelength. But this moment felt different - like Raj shared a mind with Rami. Two bodies thinking the exact same thing.

Something told Rami that this was it. This was what they were meant to do. Why they had been introduced.

What the dynamic duo found seemed evident in retrospect but eluded them when brainstorming hypotheses: the problem was how much food restaurants wasted daily. It didn't matter if the unused food in the refrigerators expired or customers only ate half of their food - the restaurant bled money either way, and the food ended up in the trash.

They agreed they couldn't solve the problem of customers not finishing their meals. No matter how sophisticated an app was, it definitely couldn't force-feed a user. At least not with current technology. But the unused food - that showed potential. That represented an inventory asset, something the company owned and must use, or it ate up profits. It was quantifiable and reportable.

So they went to work, and during one of their late-night, over-caffeinated debates, they hatched an idea: a solution for this problem was born, but required a customer portal and a restaurant control center in order to work. Rami would build an app that customers used to place orders and Raj would build a web platform that gave restaurants back-end system management.

The result: DoggyBag.

Before any ingredients went rotten, a restaurant could cook up a random meal using food nearing expiration - but not expired yet. Then they report to DoggyBag how many meals they made on the system. They could set their own prices for these DoggyBags, and users could buy dinners from restaurants at a price much lower than was on the menu. Pick up a DoggyBag before the restaurant closed, and you could have a top-rated meal for under $100.

In the beginning, customers had to pick up

their meals themselves. But after Crain's featured DoggyBag in their issue about hot local startups, he began getting calls. The first significant offer came from Uber. They wanted to become their exclusive delivery partner. Darrell's money came knocking soon after. And it was significant. He could wield real power with his shares. But he assured them that Rami would remain CEO, Raj COO, and they would remain majority shareholders.

Looking back at this time now, Rami's foolishness is crystal clear to him. He often wishes for the life he would have had if they had not taken Darrell's money. But who could he ever say this to? From everyone else's point of view, he had everything. And he did.

But not quite.

❖

Brooke first saw the news of Rami's AMA in her Twitter feed when some internet troll tagged her. Tagged her new account, that is. The tweet referenced her as the terminator of Rami's professional - and personal, it seemed - life.

"Rami is doing an Ask Me Anything?" Brooke said to herself, unaware she'd said it out loud.

It occurred to her that she had not thought

about Rami in quite some time. The guilt stopped her in her tracks. What did it say about her that she could destroy someone's life and then just... move on?

She couldn't remember what she was doing before getting the Twitter notification. Where even was she?

In a grocery store. That's right, she thought to herself with a second of hesitation. What am I here to buy? After standing in an aisle for an eternity, unaware of the shopping cart by her side, she walked out of the store.

When she got to the sidewalk, she pulled up the tweet and reread it. This time, she focused more on the news of Rami's AMA than the backhanded reminder to the public of how she was involved in the dissolution of his world.

Why? popped into her head. And then it suddenly felt like her blood pressure had dropped. She was deflating. Her stomach churned. She began sweating.

Was Rami going to try to take her down? Was this how he would exact revenge? Had he finally stewed on what happened long enough that he decided to take her down with him?

While this is precisely what will happen, it is undoubtedly not Rami's intention. Nor does it even occur to him that Brooke could somehow be a casualty of his AMA. While he thought about her and their meeting constantly for months, she never crossed his mind for even a second after he read Raj's email.

Of course, Brooke couldn't possibly know this without contacting Rami - something her editor and the publisher's lawyers insisted she avoids. So there she stood, sweating and woozing on Halsted as her imagination ran wild with possible outcomes - each more terrible than the last.

She decided to head home and lay down.

While she walked to her apartment, she logged into her old work email account. The Tribune gave her a new one they deemed more difficult to guess when her original email became nothing more than a hoarder's smorgasbord of requests to comment. It had been months since she was in here. And she held her breath as her inbox loaded.

Thanks to the AMA announcement, the vultures were back. Over 100 new emails in the last 24 hours. From a variety of publications.

Oh shit, she thought. Here we go…

Darrell's choice to simply show up at Rami's rather than call him told Rami that there was something serious he wanted to discuss. And it wasn't hard to guess that it was related to the AMA announcement.

He doesn't hear from Darrell in nearly 10 months, and now he wants to drop by to say hi. Interesting, Rami thought.

He debated buzzing Darrell up. Maybe I'll pretend I'm not home, he thought.

Everyone knows you never leave the house, you idiot, he scolded his introverted instincts. What do I have to lose?

He let Darrell up and poured himself some more coffee.

"Rami," Darrell said with a strange pain in his voice before giving him an unexpected hug. Like they were old friends. Brothers in arms.

"Hi, Darrell. Coffee?"

"Um," Darrell said and then paused. Rami enjoyed watching the gears turn as Darrell tried to figure out how to proceed when clearly he hoped this would be a brief visit. "Sure!"

Shit, thought Rami.

Okay - so what followed was an excruciating 30-minute exercise in banal non-conversation accompanied by more-frequent-than-not awkward pauses. I'll spare you that part. Let's get right to it:

"So tell me about this AMA," Darrell said after one of the longer pauses - clearly uninterested in continuing the faux pleasantries.

"It was Raj's idea."

Darrell winced at the mention of Rajesh. Obviously, they didn't have a great history - what with Darrell stealing the company out from under him and getting him fired and all. He could only imagine how Raj had fed the opportunity to Rami: "You can tell your side of the story and fuck them over. Tank their share price. Humiliate Darrell and the Board."

As you know, Raj said none of this. Even if he thought it and hoped Rami would read between the lines and act on it.

"How is Raj?" Darrell asked, hoping he might suss out Raj's intentions based on Rami's response.

"He's in a really great place." Which was true.

"That's great to hear. I'm glad he's helping you get back out there."

"Thanks."

After a brief silence, Darrell dove in. "Is there anything I need to prepare for?" Rami didn't immediately answer. "That DoggyBag should prepare for?"

The answer was no. And no harm would come to DoggyBag. DoggyBag would only be brought up briefly at the start of the AMA and quickly overshadowed and forgotten completely.

For a moment, Rami debated fucking with Darrell and telling him that it would be wise to hire a crisis management PR firm.

"You don't need to worry about anything."

"Good," Darrell said with a smile. "Good!" he said, throwing back his cup of coffee. "Thank you, Rami." He got up and started to put his coat on. "I should probably head out of here. But thank you for the coffee."

Rami nodded.

"I look forward to reading the AMA," Darrell said, closing the door behind him.

Brooke woke up about two hours earlier than usual the morning of Rami's AMA.

She hadn't slept very well. It took her forever to wind down enough to go to bed, and then she couldn't fall asleep easily. Every 45 minutes or so, she would wake up thinking she had overslept, only to look at her alarm clock and realize it hadn't been that long since she last checked it.

When she woke up at 4:30, she decided to stop driving herself crazy trying to sleep. Might as well get up and start the day.

The morning proceeded in this discombobulated fashion, and Brooke entirely gave in to it. She didn't shower or get dressed for the day. She couldn't call in sick to work - because everyone knew about today's AMA and would correctly assume she wasn't ill at all, just avoiding the day. She didn't make coffee. What was the point? She didn't need help staying awake, and she didn't really need any caffeine to jack her heart rate up even more.

At around 11:00 am, she realized she couldn't remember the events of the last three or so hours. She was seated on her couch and must have just stared off into space. For hours. She couldn't remember what she had been thinking about. If anything. Probably nothing. Just waiting for the hangman.

Something needled in the back of her mind.

But whatever her brain was trying to put together, it couldn't serve up the answer just yet.

The timing of her brain's delivery couldn't have been more poorly timed. As she logged onto Reddit, a phrase slammed into her train of thought, derailing it completely, leaving her frozen: This is going to be bad.

She stared at the screen, motionless, and waited for the ax to fall.

Rami had dreaded this day his entire adult life. He'd dreaded it for most of his teenage life. Maybe all of his life? Who knows. It's amazing the mental gymnastics our minds can perform to keep us happy and sane and non-suicidal.

Sitting in front of his laptop - an open bottle of wine beside him - he readied himself.

Here we go, he thought. And posted:

I am Rami Mahmoud, Co-Founder and Former CEO of DoggyBag. Ask me anything!

My short bio: Hi, Reddit. I'm Rami Mahmoud. You probably heard of me about a year ago when my life imploded, and I was kicked out of the company I started. I haven't spoken about what happened or even spoken publicly since it happened.

This is my first AMA and the first chance to answer your questions about my side of the story.

Ask me anything!

- Rami

It only took a few minutes for the first question to appear. He let out a sigh of relief at the sheer banality of the question. Nothing explosive or worthy of virality. And the next few questions followed a similar, toothless line of questioning.

This is easier than I'd expected, Rami thought. And mere seconds later, the question he feared would be asked - knew would be asked - popped up.

You deny trying to seduce Brooke; she has stated that it never happened and was a poor choice of words. But something seems a bit fishy. The Tribune's parent company is a significant shareholder in DoggyBag and had a lot to lose if the upcoming IPO went bust. You must be able to see how it looks a little suspicious that Brooke and the Tribune tried to backpedal on her comments from that night since an actual journalistic look into the accusations could put the IPO at risk. So why should we believe any of you?

Rami stood up from his computer. He couldn't

wait too long to respond - every minute he didn't respond was one more minute for the idea's claws to sink into the minds of other readers.

His phone pinged. He picked it up and saw a text from Raj: You can tell them. I talked to Malcolm last night. Take a deep breath, don't overthink, and start typing.

I'm not going to lie. I expected this question to come up even if I hoped no one would ask. But someone was going to, and you got to it first. Congratulations. I'm sure others were trying to figure out the perfect timing to post their question so that it's the thread that goes viral.

I'm a very private person. I always have been. I was a shy kid. I am a shy adult. I had few friends and fewer who actually understood me. Now I have even fewer friends if any. And all because I spent so much of my life trying to be what I thought I needed to be rather than who I am.

I never tried to seduce or make a move on Brooke. The truth is that I am a gay, Muslim, first-generation American. I have never had a relationship with a woman, and I have never been intimate with a woman. My only romantic relationship was with Rajesh Maru, my DoggyBag co-founder. We met in college, and neither of us was out. We kept our relationship a secret from friends and family and then from investors and colleagues when we started DoggyBag. As you can probably guess from my use of past tense, we are no longer together. So it probably does not come as a big surprise that we broke up immediately after he was terminated as COO.

We often discussed coming out - maybe not to our families, but definitely to our friends. But I was almost more afraid of what the investors would say and do than my parents. And I knew how they were going to take the news. So I kept finding reasons to delay telling people until we were suddenly spending so much time apart that the conversation stopped altogether. Needless to say, I've looked at that decision a million different ways since leaving DoggyBag. Had I made a better choice, maybe everything would be okay right now. But there's very little good in playing that game. So after almost a year of playing it, I've decided to move on and accept whatever new life awaits me. Part of that moving on is finally coming to terms with my family about who I am and who I love.

My father is an only child, as was his father, and so am I. So our family line quite literally rests on me. When I told my parents last night, the first thing my father said was, "So this is the end of our family line." I explained surrogacy, but they said that didn't change anything. Even if I have a biological child, they would rather the family line end with me than that it propagates into a giant family branch of homosexuals. My mother still has not uttered a word to me.

We were such a tight-knit family when I was growing up. But things became distant and unfamiliar between us once I started to come to terms with being gay back in college. I thought I feared losing this relationship - but I've realized that I did not choose my parents, and they did not choose me, and we all deserve to live our lives to their happiest. Pretending to be the son they wanted me to be did none of us any good.

I spent nearly a year living with the consequences of inaction and not living my true self. I am done with that. I release myself of all obligations to perform for others. I will do going forward what I look back and regret not doing earlier in life. I will be my unapologetic self.

I'm taking back my life. So it doesn't matter if you believe me or not. For the first time, I have absolutely nothing to hide.

He looked at the bottle of wine. It was almost gone. Oh boy.

Brooke almost choked on her coffee when she read Rami's response to the question about trying to seduce her.

Fuck, she thought. I'm why he had to come out to his parents and destroy his relationship with them. While costing him his company. I won't be the only one who thinks this.

She wasn't. Soon, her phone began ringing, and her social media apps started pinging her with notifications.

This is it, she thought to herself.

She closed her laptop and got back in bed.

Rami's phone immediately started ringing with requests for interviews. HBO wanted to make a 3-part doc about what happened. Hulu wished to produce an original limited series recreating his story. For some reason, the podcast My Dad

Wrote a Porno reached out to see if he would be a guest on an upcoming Footnote episode.

None of this made him feel any better. He thought maybe being vindicated would help him become more extroverted. But the more people wanted to talk to him, the more he wanted to go back into hiding.

He was not made for this.

A distraction was needed. So he opened the News app on his phone to see if anyone had picked up the story. And plenty had.

As he dove deeper into the rabbit hole of opinion pieces commenting on his AMA, he drank more wine and ended up opening a second bottle.

That's when he got an idea: Why don't I go into hiding? For real. Off the grid.

He started to giggle at the idea of buying some massive acreage of land where he'd put a tiny house in the center and let the rest act as a moat holding back the real world. After a quick online search, he found a pretty amazing, enormous, old farm and ranch in Montana. Without another thought, he called his attorney. His attorney did not answer, so he left a voicemail.

"Rudyard. It's Rami. Mahmoud. I need you to

buy a property for me. Sell some of my DoggyBag shares if you need. I'm going to text you the real estate listing right now. Buy it. I don't care how much." Then he texted Michael a link to the website he had been browsing.

He wandered over to his bed, lay in it fully clothed, and fell asleep.

Chapter Five

Well, I probably don't have to tell you what happened next.

But I will. Or else I'd be an awful storyteller. I can't just assume you'll figure out everything that transpires from here on your own. Or why else am I telling you all of this?!

So here's what happened:

Brooke was canceled.

It happened with such ferocity. She found herself utterly unprepared. She thought she knew the storm coming her way based on what happened when she sent that life-changing Tweet almost a year ago. But this was worse. Much worse. Worse than she expected after reading the experiences of other people who found themselves canceled. This was ruthless. A combination of whiplash, pilates, and a sulfuric acid spray tan. Probably even worse. She probably didn't have words to describe it accurately. So she wouldn't.

Her parents tried desperately to connect with her, but the humiliation in their voices was unbearable. They called at least twice a day, every day. But she couldn't listen to her mother cry again. What could she say? That it felt like a heinous descent into hell? You can't tell your parents something like that. So she didn't. She would rush them off the phone with some excuse as to why she couldn't talk, then sit on her couch in a depressive funk and stare into space.

Social media dissected her, tore her to shreds, threw her in a food processor, and blended her into pink slime. Worse, she learned about her firing through the Tribune's response on Twitter, not from her editor. That was cool. They were so concerned with covering their asses that they couldn't even send her a fucking two-word text reading: YOU'RE FIRED. Nope, they had to tell everyone else first.

The Tribune would go on to apologize to her. Their PR and Social Media team didn't realize that she hadn't been informed and went ahead and posted the official statement. It wasn't until her editor called and notified them of the situation that they made a quick edit and removed the reference to her no longer being a member of the Tribune staff.

But it was too late. She'd already seen it. As had the world. And plenty took screenshots of it before the Tribune published the edited version. In fact, there were almost as many news stories about the Tribune biffing her firing as there were stories about her firing.

So… that was fun.

Losing her job wasn't the worst of it. At least not to her. While Rami's overwhelming onslaught of a cancelation was global, Brooke's flogging was extremely personal.

The LGBTQ+ community responded viciously. She spent her life supporting these people. She had done everything possible to be a good ally. And one shitty tweet decimated her reputation with them. Her gay and lesbian friends stopped talking to her. Even the ones who knew that she was being misrepresented had to distance themselves from her for fear of their own cancelations.

She needed to do something. She couldn't let

this be the impression most people had of her. So she decided to write an apology.

The apology she posted to Twitter and Instagram was very moving and authentic. But that didn't help. Not when she decided to open the apology with an empathetic outreach of "To my LGBTQ brothers and sisters." No sooner had she published the apology that she was getting eviscerated for not being inclusive in her opening.

The tweet that hurt the most came from one of her favorite musicians who wrote, "The fact that Brooke De los Arcos doesn't even know how to address the audience she claims to understand and love says enough. She used the whole acronym but forgot what all of the letters mean. smh."

That was just the one that hurt the most. I won't inundate you with the thousands of (even more vicious) tweets and threats of bodily harm.

There's just no winning, she finally concluded.

So she ended up deleting all of her social media accounts. She could have made them private and hidden them - but she wanted to be done with it all. She felt no need to return to social media ever again. It transformed, for her, into an unhealthy bog of eternal sadness and pain. It never made her happy. And now it was the playground of everyone who hated her with such enmity that she didn't ever want to go on it again. Everything would still be there - the internet deletes nothing. So it doesn't matter how many months or years she waits to get back on - it will all be there. Waiting for her to digest like a bottle of bleach - liquifying her insides and killing her completely.

So no. She would not participate. She would delete.

And delete she did.

Though, of course, it didn't stop anyone. And it didn't stop the news from reporting on what everyone said about her on social media. So she stopped going on the internet altogether. No watching the news. No reading the news. No engaging with the outside world in any way, shape, or form.

She felt like a prisoner in her own apartment.

Or a prisoner in her own apartment for about 35 more days, to be exact.

Yep. Her landlord cut her lease short.

Someone doxxed her, and now anyone who wanted to know where she lived could easily find out. And some fun, fine citizens of Chicago took it upon themselves to deface her apartment building facade. Over and over again. Every time the landlord cleaned it off, they made sure to correct the erasure of her public humiliation.

So it came as no surprise when she received a letter from her building's management company. Her lease was being shortened to terminate at the end of next month. They would, however, let her stay rent-free that final month - which seemed like their attempt to soften the blow. Which was… nice, she supposed. It still sucked.

How would she get another apartment? Any lease application she fills out will require her name and her last employer. Which also posed a problem - she was unemployed. Having a steady income is usually an expectation of landlords and management companies.

There were too many strikes against her. Her only option would probably be to move in with her parents. Which - basically signaled the end of everything she spent her adult life building.

Like Rami, she thought.

Rami.

She did know one single human being in her life she could talk to about all of this.

The Tribune told her not to contact him. But she no longer worked for the Tribune. Who the fuck cares what they want or don't want, she decided.

She logged onto her computer for the first time in several days. Where had she saved her notes from her interview with Rami? She had his address somewhere in there.

Found it! she celebrated for a second before her heart started racing. Am I really going to do this?

Yes. Yes, she was.

She looked at herself, wearing whatever amalgamation of comfy clothes she had randomly grabbed and tossed on this morning without giving a flying fuck.

"Yeah, that's fine," she said in the mirror.

And then, before she could second guess her decision, she headed outside and waved down a cab.

When she arrived outside his building, she almost didn't get out of the taxi. Was she crazy? Was this the most insane thing she'd ever done? Fuck it, she thought.

She didn't want Rami to deny her entry, so

when she checked in at the front desk, she lied and said she had a delivery for him. The security guard called up, and Rami said to send them up. Brooke was through and on her way up in the elevator with the press of a button.

She stepped out of the elevator and felt her feet grow cold and adhere to the floor. There she stood, about 15 or so feet from his front door, and found she simply could not move through whatever forcefield held her to her spot. So maybe she should turn around and leave? This is a terrible idea, she thought and began to turn back to the elevator.

Fortunately for us, Rami went to the door to see what was taking the delivery person so long and opened it before she had completed her about-face.

She froze. Her mind went blank for what to say.

"Brooke?"

"Mm hm," she responded, wincing at how guilty Mm hm sounded.

"Are you... dropping something off?"

"Nope." That seemed like a good enough answer to Brooke.

"Okay." He waited for her to say something.

And then it occurred to him: "Did anyone come by with a food delivery?"

She sighed. "No."

He took this in. After maybe 20 seconds, which was entirely too long, he couldn't decide if he should say something or wait for her to say something. So he waited - too long, as I said - until it felt like it had gone on too long. Which it already had - but we'll give him a pass this time. He hasn't been particularly synced up with human interaction for most of the past year.

"Do you want to… come in?" he offered.

"Do you want me to come in?" she asked and immediately regretted the sheer awkwardness of her response.

"Okay, why don't you come in." He stepped back and gestured for her to walk through his front door. Which she did. And then stopped in the entryway, awaiting further instruction. "Can I take your coat?" She handed him her coat. She still hadn't used any words yet - but that was fine. It didn't seem to be hindering her progress. However, it might be difficult to communicate her purpose for coming if she didn't start employing the

English language in at least a modicum of ways. So she blurted out:

"You were the only person I could think of who understands what I'm going through."

At this, he nodded and then opened a closet door and hung up her coat. "You want anything to drink?"

"Bourbon."

He smiled. "There's wine at my place," he said with a turn before adding, "as you know," he said with a playful jab.

"Mmmm. Yes. Yes, I do, don't I."

She waited for him to return before saying anything else. She already felt strange; she didn't want to start rambling only to find out he couldn't hear her and then have to repeat the whole embarrassing rant.

He returned carrying two bottles of the wine they had drunk previously. "I don't really know what all I own, but I know we liked this... last time."

She blurted out a laugh and then immediately recoiled with embarrassment.

"It's okay," he said, laughing.

He went to the drawer where he kept the wine

bottle opener and held it up to show her that, in at least this one way, he had grown since their last encounter. Opening the first bottle, he poured them two glasses.

"A toast: to being canceled," he offered. She took her glass and clinked it against his.

"To being canceled," she said with a smile. And then tossed the entire glass back like a shot. He stared at her, having not taken a sip yet.

With a shrug, he tossed his back as well. "I know what you mean. About understanding what you're going through. Don't take this the wrong way, but it's nice to know someone who understands after all this time dealing with it alone."

"I'm so sorry - " she started before he cut her off with a wave.

"Please don't apologize," he assured her. "Seriously. You don't need to." He gestured for her to follow him to the living room.

As he sat down, he continued: "I've actually been thinking lately that I may owe you a debt of gratitude."

She stared at him, not sure how to interpret this. Was it backhanded? Was he about to rip her to shreds? Was this all a massive error of judgment to come here?

"You forced me to leave my comfortable existence hiding from the real world and to just... embrace it. Whether I wanted to or not."

She didn't know how to respond. Was she supposed to? Was she entitled to?

"I mean, yeah - it came at a pretty brutal cost -" he started to say when he saw her wince. "But - I'm finally just... living. I don't care what I need to say or do to control what people think and know about me."

This seemed to put her at ease.

"I wish I were where you are now," she said. "I guess in, what, 11 months? Give or take? I'll be ready to rejoin the world?"

"You already did. You're here, aren't you?" She laughed. "What?"

"This is the real world?"

"This is the realest world I've ever lived in."

It was for her too. Which started to sink in a bit. "I guess you're right," she said.

She poured herself another full glass, and he took this as his cue to start opening the second.

"I thought I was fighting to gain access to the

real world. The world that Becky's and Chad's are born with access to," she said, followed by a long sip. "I worked my fucking ass off. Since... High School? Middle School? I don't know. Whenever I learned that blonde girls got what I wanted for free, and I would be unlikely ever to have it, even if I achieved wealth or fame."

He hadn't really thought much about her life. Or, to be most accurate: her. And he was suddenly overcome with a need to know her. But like most of his instincts to speak up, he ignored it.

"So how much did you see?" she finally asked, readying herself for his feelings on her downfall.

He smiled. Then laughed. "Honestly, I didn't watch any of what happened to you."

"Thank you for not wanting to watch my flaying..."

"Well, I didn't..." he started to say.

"Yes?"

"I was more afraid that watching would trigger PTSD than out of, uh, concern for you... I hope you understand."

She laughed. "Fair."

"So, how was it?" he asked with the first devilish smile she'd ever witnessed on him.

"Rude!" she yelled while smacking him. "But you did miss some fireworks. It got weeeeird at one point."

"Weirder than receiving hate mail for how you ended things with your ex-boyfriend years ago?"

"Surprisingly, yes!" Rami was speechless. "You are in the presence of perhaps the only person to ever be hated by both Fox News and MSNBC."

"Impressive accomplishment," Rami said, clinking his wine glass against hers.

"Yeah. Rachel Maddow dug into my social media history and spent an entire episode showing all of the "problematic red flags" I've been dropping along the way. Tucker Carlson did his own cursory look through my Tweets and came to the conclusion that I was a "feminist woke warrior" that the left hired to, I don't know… like take down powerful men or something. Honestly - I had a really hard time keeping track of what he was saying."

"You watched?"

"How could I not? When else would I have the chance to screengrab my name next to Tucker's grimace." Rami didn't really know how to respond correctly, so he nodded and took a sip of wine. She did as well. And awkward silence followed.

"What's next for you?" He asked, finally breaking the frozen moment.

"A homeless shelter?" she joked. And at first, he thought she was joking. Until she finished her current glass and started the first pour from Bottle #2.

"Really?!"

She stopped and looked at him with a rye smile. "Oh, you're adorable."

"What does that mean?"

"No, I'm not actually going to be homeless. I can..." She sighed before continuing, "...move in with my parents again."

"What's so bad about that?"

"Other than it's probably the most devastating thing you can do to immigrant parents who came here dreaming of a better life for you than they had?"

"One of the most devastating," he corrected. She gave him a quizzical look. "Telling your immigrant parents that you're gay when you're the 'end of the family line' is pretty high up there."

"Oof. Yeah. Yours is worse than mine," she said with faux seriousness.

"Shut up!" he tried to say with conviction before erupting into drunken laughter.

This is such a lovely moment to witness. The two of them happy. Experiencing actual happiness, not Hallmark Channel happiness. For Rami, it's been almost a year. Though it's arguable if he has been happy for even one moment since he and Raj broke up. And Brooke can't claim that her happiness this past year was authentic. Even if she was trying to keep it in the very back of her mind, she never stopped feeling the guilt of destroying Rami's life. It was there like an itch every time she thought she was happy. So this is probably the only time the two have ever shared real joy with another human being since they lost their childhood innocence.

I'm sorry to say that while I'd love to let us bask in this happiness for as long as possible, this scene is nearly coming to an end. And not one I have any control over. This is all their doing. Even a storyteller can't fight the gravitational slumber of alcohol-infused human beings. So let's wrap this up. Because what you're really here for is tomorrow's phone call. But hold that thought.

Rami's phone vibrated. It was the front desk again.

"Hello?"

"Mr. Mahmoud, there are… well, it looks like a group, but they don't seem to be together…"

Reporters, Rami guessed with perfect accuracy.

"They've asked for you, but I keep telling them you're not home right now. What do you want me to do?"

"Thanks, Ivan. Just stick with I'm not home."

"Got it. Have a nice night, sir."

"Goodnight, Ivan. And thank you again." Rami ended the call.

"It looks like you're crashing here tonight."

Brooke wasn't on the couch. Where was she?

"Then I guess we'll need a third bottle," she said, coming around the corner.

They didn't actually finish the third bottle. They maybe had half a glass each before passing out on the couch.

When Rami's phone rang the third time, he finally answered it.

"Who is this?" he asked, his voice husky. He coughed and reached for some water. But there were only half-filled wine glasses around him. So he grabbed a glass and threw it back. Which was awful. So he coughed it up and made an absolute mess. Which startled Brooke awake.

"Rami?"

"Yeah?"

"It's Rudyard."

Why the fuck is my attorney calling me this early?, his brain managed to piece together.

"What time is it?"

"Um. Four in the afternoon." Rami's eyes snapped open.

"Oh, whoa. Okay." Rami said without thought. Then it occurred to him he had no idea why he was on the phone with his attorney. "Wait. What?"

"It's four -" his attorney began before Rami cut him off.

"No, what are you calling for?"

"The sale closed this morning, and I've sent scans of the paperwork to your personal email."

"What sale?"

Now, Rami couldn't see his attorney, so he was not aware of this: but at that moment, his attorney took his phone away from his ear to make sure he had called the correct number. For a full three seconds, Rami had, by complete accident, gaslit his attorney into thinking maybe he'd accidentally called the wrong Rami Mahmoud in his client base.

Except he didn't have any other clients named Rami Mahmoud. So his attorney did what humans often do when they are baffled: he shook his head. I'm not sure why we do that. It's not like we can dislodge synapses with a jog of the ol' cranium.

He spoke a little slower: "The property in Montana?" Rami had no response. "That you asked me to purchase for you?" Rami still had no idea what he was talking about. So he did the perfectly normal human head-shaking routine. And by sheer coincidence - Rami dislodged a synapse teetering on the edge of thought and suddenly remembered.

"Oh! Wait. Closed on the sale?"

"Yes. And the documents are in your email."

Rami put his attorney on speakerphone and scrambled to pull up his email. "Tell me about this property…"

"The one you asked me to buy?"

"That's the one," Rami said, not really listening.

"I was able to negotiate it down to about fifty million. A little less than fifty."

This made Brooke's eyes snap open. What are they talking about? she thought.

Even Rami stopped for a second. I just spent fifty million dollars...

"The farmhouse has seven bedrooms and three bathrooms. There are two grain silos on the property. Three commercial barns-"

Rami cut him off, "Okay. And it's in..."

"Montana. North of Bozeman."

Brooke and Rami looked at each other. Neither knew what to say. But both were thinking the same thought: This sounds like a fun adventure.

"Thanks, Rudyard," he said before smiling at Brooke. "Can you book me a private jet to Montana and then a helicopter from that airport to the property?"

"I'm not a travel agent," Rudyard started to push back. But then he thought better, "It's going on your monthly invoice. I'll text you in a moment with the address of the airfield. And then he ended the call.

"You're looking for somewhere to live, right?"

"Yeah, in Chicago."

"Because…?"

"Because… no reason," she admitted.

And that's how it came to be that Brooke took her first flight on a private jet for her first visit to the State of Montana, where she would live in her first farmhouse with a man whose life she destroyed by accident and who, in return, accidentally destroyed hers.

INTERLUDE

Okay! We've made it through their first year!

I'm sorry I had to put you through all of that. Both Brooke and Rami will tell you that was the worst of it. Honestly - it gets weirder from here, but they don't hit rock bottom again. At least, not that I know of. They're not even 40 yet, so I suppose there may be at least one more period of darkness waiting for both of them, individually or together. I intend to check in with them now and then, so I'm happy to update you should anything interesting, positive or negative, head their way.

Now - here's what I wanted you to see before I tell you about Brooke and Rami's second year:

Let's saunter over to the roadblock Ralph and his friends have set up. A couple of tips: don't avoid eye contact - that makes you suspicious to these guys. Instead, look them in the eye and nod. Show solidarity with them, and they'll assume you're on their side.

As we get closer, you'll notice that there are no utility poles or power lines leading down the main road into the property. When the locals started fussing enough to make threats, Rami concluded that it was only a matter of time before they decided to send a signal by taking down their access to power. And he was wise to come to this conclusion as they did indeed do just that some seven or so weeks later. Fortunately for the people living on the property, Rami replaced their dependence on an external power supply by building a solar farm in one of the empty fields adjacent to the farmhouse. When Dickie and Bart Mulford got their friends Wyatt and Willy - twin brothers Bart grew up and rarely socialized with but who owned a cherry picker - to join their merry band of saboteurs and cut the wires at every pole, it didn't matter.

In fact, Rami took great joy in removing the poles so that the Mulfords and their clan could see how they did him a favor in some ways.

Boy, did Bart and Dickie get the message.

When they drove by and saw the crews removing the poles, the surprise caused Dickie to fumble his lit cigarette and send it careening down his shirt.

Livid and nursing a burned belly button, he sped down to Don's to tell everyone, "those shame-towners are fucking mocking us!"

And he wasn't wrong.

Rami would eventually admit - last month, actually - that he should never have responded that way. He could have just ignored them. They were already energy independent at that time. There was no need to give them the middle finger.

But he wanted to. And it felt good. So he did.

And the cold war that ensued was set in motion.

We're not going to stay near the roadblock - that may spook them into thinking we intend to get onto the property.

That hill over and to the left is our destination. From there, you can use binoculars to see more of the other buildings.

While we make our way over there - and I do apologize for all the walking - I'm going to let you in on something no one sees coming. I promise not to ruin anything for you! Just a teaser:

Exactly nine hours, forty-seven minutes, and

twenty-two seconds ago, a car set off from Boise, Idaho, headed for this very spot. While the driver of the vehicle will be surprise enough for the fine folks defending this blockade, the contents of the car is the real surprise.

Depending on how many rest stop breaks were taken and whether or not an overnight stay was necessary - I'm expecting the car to arrive within the next two or three hours. And you're not going to want to miss it.

If you need to take a breather, take it. If not, point your binoculars at that big tree way in the distance and zoom in until you can see the house.

The farmhouse is pretty much the only building on the property that still resembles its original self from when Rami bought the land. The other original buildings have been repurposed.

Behind and to the right of the farmhouse, you'll see one of the barns has been painted blue. That's what they call the General Store. But it's more like a co-op. I don't know what to call it. But basically: Rami buys essentials in bulk from distributors or directly from the source and sells everything at exactly 10% more than he pays for it, and the neighbors, as they've come to call themselves, can purchase these essentials. Now, if a neighbor prefers a different brand of toilet paper, they are more than welcome to do their own shopping back where the roads are paved. And some did choose to do just that once a month. But none of the carriers - not even the United States Postal Service - would deliver to the property. All deliveries came in through a freight company, whose cost was paid for by some of the 10% he charged.

The barn that's straight ahead of us is called the Community Center. As its name suggests, it's where the community gathers whenever there is a need. It has started to be used on the weekends as a sort of informal church. Something neither Rami nor Brooke had ever imagined. Though, if you ask one of the neighbors, they'll tell you that the night the barn was transformed for the wedding of Anya and Jeff was the first time anyone called the barn beautiful. And it was. Anya was a party decorator, after all. Or had been until the whole gay wedding incident.

The silos... the silos are interesting. They were Rami's first real change to the property.

And the locals took note.

Something like that meant these people weren't

planning to leave anytime soon. At the same time, more seemed to be rolling in every week or so.

"We've been patient," George said after a few High Lifes down at Don's. "Even when the press first came, we didn't say or do nothing." Everyone agreed with this.

"Let's go have a talk with those two," Ralph said from his usual table. "Apparently, we didn't make ourselves clear the first time."

That was the conversation that led to the meeting with Rami and Brooke that led to Dickie, Bart, Wyatt, and Willie cutting the power lines to the property led to Rami's cheeky replacement of the now-useless utility poles with flower gardens that led to the cold war between the locals and the neighbors that led to Ralph's ruin.

Damn silos.

But before we jump into that, let's take one last swing by Ralph as I want you to hear his exact words when he finally listens to the voicemail that he didn't listen to when the number he didn't recognize called him some nine hours, forty-nine minutes, and thirty-one seconds ago.

Yep, he's listening to it as we speak. And:

"Fuck...Oh... fuck."

PART
TWO

ONE YEAR AGO

Chapter Six

I have a video I want you to watch. At this point, unfortunately, it's a YouTube Classic. It appeared on numerous Best Of lists, won a Webby, and been seen on every talk show around the globe.

This was before phone cameras got really good - so as it zooms in, it does get a little grainy. But don't worry - it's one piece of a compilation of videos. You'll get to see the real action.

Okay, so you're looking at Wrigley Field from behind home plate.

World Series. Seventh game. Final inning. Brewers up by one point.

The Brewers' second time at the World Series. They haven't been back in decades. And they're favored to win.

Two outs. Two strikes. Bases loaded.

Brewers need one more out, and the series is theirs.

Now keep your eye on the Brewers' right fielder.

The pitch... the bat makes contact... the ball flies!

And there, the Brewers' right fielder realizes there's a chance he can catch the ball. He sprints for it.

From way back here, you can see him jump, reach as far as he can stretch, come back to earth...

And throw his glove on the ground.

The players on the field watch in silence as the merry-go-round of their opponents spins around the bases.

The Brewers lose by 3 points.

Game over.

But let's look at that again from a closer vantage point.

See the stately, older woman sitting there next to that scrawny young boy - those are our friends Willye and Wilson. Well, they're not our friends yet - their lives are still in perfectly good working order at this moment. It's in less than 30 seconds that their world will end.

You see Willye point - she grabs Wilson by the shoulder. The boy stands up, his glove ready. He reaches as far as he can stretch, dips the glove, and...

He caught it! Willye immediately starts to hug him... and that's where the video begins to get shaky. You can see the people around them screaming. Willye even has to hit some of them with her purse to keep them back. A man in his 50s grabs the ball out of Wilson's hand and throws it back on the field.

Now we flip over to the most famous clip of this moment:

Across from us, you can see Willye and Wilson sitting. She grabs his shoulder and points. You can see the right fielder sprinting to the wall. He jumps, he and Wilson both reach as far as they can stretch, and just as the ball is about to land snuggly in his glove, a newer-looking glove dips down and over and catches it, pulling the ball from the right fielder's opportunity to win the series. The others seated around Willye and Wilson start to crowd them, and then you see the ball get flung back to the field.

Here's the clip that the late-night hosts simply loved:

We're zoomed in on the right fielder as he comes back down to the ground and looks at his empty glove before tearing it off and throwing it down.

Then, the right fielder sees the ball soar over his head and land about 10 feet in front of him. He kicks at it and misses before walking away in a huff.

The late shows enjoyed layering the sad Charlie Brown melody underneath. The one we always hear when Charlie Brown is walking away in shame, head down.

Lastly - here's how this moment was used as a meme:

On the left side of the image is a still of Wilson smiling, reaching for the ball as Willye smiles beside him. On the right side is a still of Willye wielding her purse as Wilson cries beside her.

Most who shared it considered it witty.

Willye and Wilson considered it a non-stop reminder of how their lives will never be the same.

I haven't told you about Randle. Yes, it's spelled

like "handle." His mom was worried people would misspell it if she spelled it the usual way, so she misspelled it for them. Oddly enough, everyone misspells his name R-A-N-D-A-L-L.

He's a happy person - a very happy person, actually - but most people wouldn't guess that because he doesn't smile much. Or ever. Or talk much, for that matter. You see, he's one of those handsome All-American boys, except his teeth are a trainwreck. His mom raised him on her own, so there were no funds for braces. (He was lucky if there were funds to see a doctor for an ear infection.) Since he doesn't talk much, he has learned to fade into the background and be ignored. And then he observes. He likes to people-watch. It's why he wanted this job. It's also why he was the only one to spot the helicopter coming.

Randle works at the diner where Rayray's wife works. Well, not wife yet. They're engaged. And have been since High School. Which was many years ago. But that doesn't stop Charlene from calling him her husband. So everyone thinks they're married. The only two who know they aren't are Rayray and Charlene.

Charlene was in the back on break, and Randle

was wiping down the menus at a table in the front. No one was patronizing the establishment at this moment, so there were no distractions to prevent Randle from staring out the front window. Which is where he was staring when he saw the shadow of a helicopter float up the road in front of the diner.

Putting down the menus, he darted outside to see what had made such a shadow. And sure enough, it was a helicopter.

He stood in the middle of the street, watching it fly into the distance toward the old ranch out that way. Even when it disappeared, he kept watching. He didn't need to worry about such things as getting hit by a car as there weren't that many people driving around here at this time of the day. He probably would still be standing there if Charlene didn't return from her break to find three people waiting to be seated. While apologizing to them for the wait, she spotted Randle in the street, looking up at the sky like a turkey.

"Randle!"

Randle blinked hard and rubbed his eyes. His eyes were dried out from not blinking for however long he stood there, not blinking.

"Randle! What are you doing?!" Charlene shouted from the diner.

"A helicopter!" he shouted back. Which made absolutely no sense to Charlene since she hadn't seen anything.

She rolled her eyes and went back inside. He can find his own way out of the middle of the street, she thought to herself.

She grabbed three menus from the clean pile where Randle had been working and sat the patrons at a table near the front windows.

"Did you see that helicopter?" one of the women asked Charlene.

"What?!" Charlene shouted. Randle actually saw a helicopter? she thought with surprise.

This scared the shit out of the woman who had spoken. Not only because of the volume Charlene shouted at, but because she's a rather imposing figure at 6' 1". She's as tall as Rayray. And you won't see her in a dress outside of a formal setting - she never entirely grew out of her tomboy phase. Though she did finally give in to Rayray's pleading with her to grow her hair out after she tried a pixie cut. You can still see the blonde tips of the pixipocalypse lightening her natural sandy red color. Charlene could only have descended from the women who survived the Oregon Trail. If anyone could have shot 100 lbs of squirrels and carried all of it, it would be one of Charlene's ancestors.

"A helicopter is heading out to the old cattle ranch!" Randle shouted as he came back into the diner.

"A helicopter..." Charlene turned over in her head.

"What's the soup of the day?" one of the ladies asked.

"Um..." Charlene mumbled before realizing she wasn't answering.

"Broccoli cheddar," she offered as soon as it popped into her head.

"I'll take that with the number 14, hold the tomato," the woman replied.

Charlene pulled out her notepad and started jotting down the order.

And like that, she forgot all about the mystery of the helicopter.

Neither Rami nor Brooke ever visited a ranch

before today. Nor had they ever been in a farmhouse.

But they found themselves now standing outside a farmhouse on the ranch that Rami now owned and were steeling themselves before crossing the threshold and officially making this their new life.

"Shall we?" Rami gestured towards the porch.

"I like your porch," she said.

"Thank you. Growing up, I'd always wanted one."

"Really?"

"God no. Can you imagine how many spiders are hiding in the corners?" he joked. And then he actually gave the thought a moment and shivered.

Brooke burst out laughing. "Did you just give yourself the willies?"

He joined in, laughing with embarrassment, before grabbing her hand.

Now, they were completely unaware of what these next few steps would lead to. They did not end at the mere entrance to a farmhouse. No, these steps led to an entirely new way of life. Over the next year, they would solve problems they never imagined, let alone prepared for, and meet people whose paths they would never have crossed had they not chosen to reset their lives here in this farmhouse in Montana. But take these steps they did, ignorant as they were to their futures, and in the house they went, sealing their fate with the - entirely appropriate - bang of a screen door.

They would need to start with furniture. The bare, wooden floors wore scars where the previous owner's tables and chairs and couch sat for much of the floor boards' existence.

Existence as floorboards that is. They enjoyed a delightfully full life as a beech tree back before people cleared this area of trees, preparing it for raising cattle.

The beech tree really didn't see it as a problem, being a beech tree - it was a beech tree, after all. Nonetheless, the beech tree had been retired from its tree duties and reassigned to a less dangerous job than the wilds of the outdoors: indoor flooring. Yes, this lucky beech tree had been set aside by the man - who was the man of the family he was man of - when the gents and woman clearing the trees asked him what he wanted to do with them after they ripped them from the ground.

"I'll keep the ones with orange circles around them," he instructed the woman and gents.

And this beech happened to be one with one of these life-saving circles encompassing it.

Or you might mistake it as life-saving when, in fact, it simply indicated which pile to put it in after being ripped from the soil. Which is what this beech tree's circle indicates, much to my disappointment. I thought surely this was his system for picking out the trees he wished to keep alive and growing on the property. But - no. He planned to use the orange-encircled trees as wood for the interior of the house he planned to build on this spot.

Rami, of course, would never know this story, so neither would Brooke, as he would not tell it to her. It's a part of the story that only you and I know.

So without comment on the floor boards' origin, our heroic duo stood in the foyer. Rami flipped the light switch next to the door frame. The bulb in the lamp above their heads made that little popping noise light bulbs make when they die. Their tiny death scream, paffing as it blinks out of existence.

"Add new lightbulbs to the list," Brooke said with a smile.

"Maybe an electrician too, while we're building a list of things to acquire," Rami mused.

They made their way into the kitchen. A large open space with an enormous island in the center of the room. The sink looked like it could be repurposed as a bathtub if need be; it was so deep and spanned the length of half the outside-facing wall.

Rami opened the cupboards two at a time. All were empty until he got to the ones in the pantry, just slightly out of reach.

Good old-fashioned Maxwell House coffee. He pulled the container down and popped it open. It smelled exactly like cheap coffee, but it didn't smell stale or rotten. Brooke smelled it from across the room: "Oh my god. I would love a cup of coffee," Brooke sighed. Rami looked and felt around for coffee filters.

Brooke found a pot inside the oven. "I'll start boiling the water."

"I don't think we have filters," Rami responded.

"Hm," Brooke said before wandering off without explanation.

Rami continued to look for coffee filters in drawers and the high shelves of the pantry while Brooke was opening the linen closet door in the bathroom nearest to the kitchen.

She returned with a roll of toilet paper. "This should work," she said with forced optimism. You know the kind of forced optimism that fuels you before your first cup of coffee. When you have no reason to live, and there is no justification for getting out of bed but, by golly, you must., You must! Or else will?! This is the existential gauntlet every coffee addict chooses to compete in or not each time they awaken to the world of the living.

They both stood there for a moment in silence, trying to figure out what step came next and why they couldn't remember said step.

"Did you see a coffee maker anywhere?" Rami asked Brooke with no optimism at all. This was another common reaction to not having consumed any coffee since waking.

"No," she replied. Then something caught her eye, up on top of the cabinets. "Is that a vase?"

Rami turned and looked. He couldn't see anything, so he hopped on the counter. Sure enough, it was a vase.

He handed her the vase and then hopped down. They looked at it for a second before Brooke started to layer toilet paper on top of it. He scooped the coffee grounds into the homemade toilet paper cone Brooke had constructed so carefully.

As Brooke started pouring the boiling water over the grounds - Rami laughed.

"What? Am I doing it wrong?"

He laughed harder before explaining: "I was just thinking: a year ago, would you have ever thought you'd be standing here doing this with me now?"

Without hesitation, she answered, "Fuck, no!"

See? I told you.

With the workday long done and the sun down, Ray's little tribe would soon be down at Don's soaking up their fill of cheap beer and tobacco until they, like sponges, can absorb no more, and they, like sponges, must relieve themselves of their bladdatory burden, and thus the establishment of themselves.

It was still early, though, and so while their judgment had most certainly been impaired, it was not nearly impaired enough not to order another beer. An ideal state for them to inhabit when Charlene came in to join them.

Not a word had been spoken about the Mystery of the Helicopter and the Old Ranch - as I would have called it if I was writing a hardboiled detective pulp potboiler, which this is not and will not be. This was to be expected, though, as the only people who witnessed or heard about it were not presently in Don's.

That is, however, going to change soon. In fact, very soon.

"The corporate elite are who pull the strings here, not the government," Rayray explained to the group. "Politicians want us to think they are in charge, so they put up a big show about fighting over bills and filibustering and trying to jam bills through reconciliation!"

Bart and Dickie were now completely lost. They followed along with him until he got to "filibustering" - at which point, they were so busy trying to remember what filibustering is that they completely missed the part about reconciliation. Which is probably for the best - it would have confused them even more.

I don't tell you any of this because I think you

should know what any of this means. I'm not sure I do. But that is irrelevant because Rayray does, and he's who's speaking.

Breaking his long silence, Ralph spoke up and grabbed everyone's attention.

"The elite leave us alone," Ralph said after a sip of beer. He wiped the foam from his mustache before continuing. "They don't want this place. We don't have anything to offer that they want."

"You sure about that?" Rayray needled Ralph.

Ralph leaned toward Rayray and made eye contact: "Why would they leave their fancy beaches and cities? Why would they choose Montana over San Francisco? Why would they leave Ssilicone Vvalley?"

"Silicon Valley?" Rayray corrected him, "It's not silicone -"

"I don't care what it is," Ralph interrupted. "They've got their place. We've got ours. There's no reason for us to go there. There's no reason for them to come here."

"What did my husband stir up now?" Charlene asked as she came over and sat on the bar stool next to Rayray. Charlene took Rayray's ball cap off his head, smacked him with it, sniffed it, rolled her eyes at the gang to show how awful it smelled, and then put it back on his head backwards. Everyone laughed, as they always do. Everyone loves Charlene. She reminds every man in town of their mama. And she does mother all of them.

"Why'd you assume I stirred up something?" Rayray asked her with a smile. See? Even Rayray didn't seem to remember that they weren't actually married. Now that I think about it, Charlene has employed some truly next-level reverse psychology here.

She rolled her eyes at him and then went in for a kiss. "I was simply explaining to the guys… Ya know what? Nevermind." And then, for effect, he stood up and said, "Nevermind," before sitting back down.

"How were pie sales today, Charlene?" Bart asked with a tinge of hope in his voice. Bart, you see, had a sweet tooth. But not a lot of money. And it was well known throughout the county that Charlene made some of the best baked goods you could buy. Which made them a little more expensive than Bart could afford.

Fortunately for Bart, Charlene decided, through an utterly chaotic series of events driven by geographical proximity and happenstance, that she would marry his older brother Rayray. And while they never technically married, she seemed to be the only one who knew that, so she treated him exactly as she would her brother-in-law: as a family member. And fortunately for Bart, she believed that family is essential and you should take care of your family. So she always saves one of the left-over baked goods at the end of the day and brings it to Don's for Bart.

"I'm sorry to say everyone wanted pie today, Bart," she said with a gentle lilt. Bart shrugged to express, No big deal. "I wish I could say the same about brownie sales," she said with a smile as she pulled a square of chocolate-infused delight. She tossed it to Bart, who blew her a kiss as thanks.

This then became one of those moments that the family had grown to experience more and more frequently as Bart aged: he would do some-thing effeminate and then continue with his life - oblivious to the stares of everyone else. Every-one would look at each other. Eventually, one of them would shrug, and everyone would shrug in response, and then they'd all forget about it and move on.

Charlene didn't forget, though. She remembered. She remembered Bart as a little kid when she was his babysitter, and the games he liked and the toys he would want to play with. And how he'd ask her, "You won't tell Dad?" when she let him put on her lipstick and eye shadow.

As everyone else stared at Bart, she smiled at him, hoping some part of him would pick up her signal. The signal she was trying to send said I see you.

He didn't get the signal.

While retrieving and reviewing these teenage memories of Bart as a child, she remembered the incident when his father arrived home early one night and noticed a lipstick kiss imprinted on the white cloth parachute of the action figure Bart held in his hand. It was the one thing Charlene forgot to clean up before his parents returned.

His father ripped the action figure out of his hand, held it above his head, and then dropped it. The kiss stood out brightly for all to see - shouting his transgression to the whole world. The shame she remembered seeing on his face as the shadow of the parachute played across his frozen expression.

As is often the case, this completely tangential, unrelated memory caused a few synapses in her brain to make a wild leap and draw a connection between the shadow on Bart's face as a child and the helicopter shadow Randle had mentioned. And as is also often the case when one experiences a wild leap of imagination popping into view, Charlene said, "Oh!" catching everyone's attention.

"Randle saw a helicopter today," she said with matter-of-fact indifference.

The guys - paranoid as they can be - did not show any indifference to this subject or its implications. Quite the contrary. They immediately grew highly suspicious.

"Saw a helicopter?" Rayray asked. "Where?"

"At the diner," she said with the same matter-of-fact neutrality.

"There was a helicopter at the diner?" Bart asked.

"Bart…" Rayray said, more to himself than Bart.

"No, it was flying past. Up toward the old ranch. Or at least that's where he thinks it was headed."

The sound of a zippo Zippo lighter flicking open rang. Everyone looked to Ray. He was the only one who used a zippoZippo. "Sounds like we should pay these tourists a visit," he said definitively.

Ray rarely spoke. But when he did, everyone listened, and nobody argued.

After a few seconds, Dickie stood up and pulled on his jacket, "Alright, let's go."

Rayray kissed Charlene on the cheek while the others finished their beers and followed them to their trucks.

Brooke and Rami wandered the property for about four hours after spending a couple of hours exploring the house.

Looking at his watch, Rami commented, "We should head back to the helicopter soon."

She struggled to lift one of the timbers that made up the fence they were walking along. "Oh my god. I can't believe someone lifted these to build this fence," she said, panting. "I'm not a weakling, you know."

"I would never take you for one," Rami answered.

The fence they were walking along turned from wood to metal. "This must be the front gate to the property," Rami concluded as they reached a large box with a mechanism attached to the chainlink. As they continued down the fence, a set of tracks appeared on the ground, and they could see that the section of chainlink attached to the mechanism was resting on a set of small wheels that, in turn, rested on the tracks.

Eventually, they came to the other end of the chainlink and saw that it joined up with another piece of metal fencing with some sort of springloaded lever. Brooke impulsively triggered the lever, and the chainlink started to roll sideways, leaving behind it a large opening across an expanse of unpaved road.

Well, it made it about 18 inches before it ground to a halt.

Rami and Brooke looked at each other. Brooke grabbed hold of the end of the chainlink and pulled it back to where it had been latched. She once again triggered the lever, but nothing happened.

"You broke it," Rami deadpanned.

"I did not!"

Rami shrugged before giving in to the laugh he was holding back. "This seems easy enough," he said, grabbing the chainlink with both hands and trying to roll it open. It moved, but only with great effort.

"Very easy!" Brooke mocked him.

"Do you hear that?" Rami asked, not giving Brooke the reaction she wanted.

"What?"

"Listen."

They stood quietly until both saw a set of headlights in the distance. And then another set. And then another.

"Visitors," Rami said, trying not to sound worried. However, it didn't matter if he sounded worried or not to Brooke because it didn't worry her in the slightest.

"Guess we'll get to meet our new neighbors," Brooke said, confident and a little excited.

The two exchanged no other words while they watched the headlights nearing. When finally Ray's truck came over the hill and approached the gate, he pulled over about 50 feet from the gate. Ralph's truck - with Rayray riding shotgun - pulled up behind Ray's, and Dickie's truck - with Bart riding shotgun - continued past the other two trucks because they were too busy arguing over who owed who a pack of Parliament Lights to notice that the others had stopped.

"Dickie!" Bart yelled when he saw they were on track to drive through a fence. Dickie reacted in enough time to come to a screeching halt before they hit the fence. Staring into their headlights stood two people they had never seen before in their lives.

Or at least, they didn't remember seeing them. They undoubtedly saw their photos a year ago when you couldn't go 24 hours without some social media hysterics about Rami. But that was almost a year ago, and besides - it had absolutely nothing to do with them and had zero impact on their lives, so rather than tucking their images into a pocket of their mind for future retrieval, their brains chose to forget.

To their surprise, neither Brooke nor Rami flinched as they watched Dickie's truck hurtling towards them. Both had faced the end of their lives as they knew them. Getting splattered by a truck would be par for the course.

Brooke waved.

"Sorry!" Dickie shouted out the driver's window.

"That's okay," Rami replied.

Dickie was confused. He'd been apologizing to Ray. But rather than explaining, he waved instead.

Ray passed Dickie's truck on the passenger side while Ralph came around on the driver's side. Rayray had stayed in the truck.

"Evening," Ralph offered the strangers. "I'm Ralph. We live in the town back there," he said, nodding in the direction of the town. Though it definitely wasn't the direction of the town. Anytime Ralph nodded in the direction of town, he always indicated that it was to his left. At this very moment, it was actually behind him.

"I'm Rami," he said, extending his hand through the fence.

"Brooke," she said with a wave.

To Rami's surprise, it was actually Ray who took his hand and shook it. He could feel that Ray was giving him the kind of firm handshake you give someone when you're trying to determine if you can beat them up or not. Rami squeezed back. Not hard enough to let Ray know he knew what he was doing, but enough to surprise Ray with its firmness.

"Ray."

"I'm Dickie, and this is my brother Bart," Dickie offered from his truck window.

"Nice to meet you all," Rami said, Ray still gripping his hand.

"Here on vacation?" Ralph asked, trying not to imbue the question with any sense of suspicion.

Brooke and Rami looked at each other and then laughed. It occurred to both of them simultaneously that they had not been recognized. These guys didn't indicate that they recognized Rami or Brooke. At that moment, they shared the same thought: Looks like this was the right place to move to after all.

That, of course, would not be how they felt in a few months.

"Well, actually..." Rami didn't know exactly how to say that they were moving in.

"We're moving in," said Brooke.

Rami shrugged to himself.

"You bought the ranch?" Ray asked.

Rami was relieved that Ray had released his hand with that question. "Uh, yes. Yesterday actually."

Ray nodded but said nothing in response.

"What brings you here?" asked Ralph.

"We wanted to get out of the city," Brooke answered. Which was true, even if it wasn't the truth.

"Bozeman?" Ralph asked, knowing that this would not be their answer.

"Chicago," Rami and Brooke said in unison.

They all then stood in silence. Rami wanted to break it in the hopes it would end the interaction, and they could get back to the helicopter and back to Chicago.

"We'd open the gate for you, but it seems stuck," Rami blurted out.

Ralph nodded and walked up to the fencing. Looking down at the tracks, he made his way to the box with the mechanism.

"Ray, on three, lift that gate about an inch," Ralph shouted back to the group. He took hold of the chain that had slipped off. "One, two, three!" As Ray lifted the gate, the gear the chain was supposed to be attached to leaned close enough that he could quickly loop it over and fit it over the teeth.

Without warning, the mechanism snapped into action, and the gate was pulled out of Ray's hands, landing back on its tracks with enough of a rattle and bang that Brooke screamed.

"That should do the trick," Ralph said as he neared them again. "But you'll need to get that fixed permanently. The gear is wobbly. The chain will keep slipping off until it's tightened."

"Thank you," Rami shouted over the sound of the opening gate.

"No problem, it's what neighbors do," Ralph said. "Well, welcome to the neighborhood," he said before heading back to his truck.

The sound of Ray's zippo Zippo opening and igniting a flame stole Rami and Brooke's attention from Ralph's exit. Ray lit a cigarette and then nodded at them before turning around and heading to his truck.

As they watched the headlights shrink into the distance, Rami and Brooke worked together to pull the gate back into its closed and locked position. When it was locked, they said nothing to each other. In silence, they turned and headed back to the helicopter.

Watching Brooke and Rami fade away in his rearview mirror, Ralph felt a realization coming together in his mind.

"So who are they?" asked Rayray.

And that's when the realization clicked. "They, Rayray, are your corporate elite."

❖

When Ray, Ralph, Rayray, Dickie, and Bart returned to Don's, they were greeted by Charlene behind the bar, wiping it down.

"What can I get you boys?" she asked in her best Don imitation. Which was actually quite good!

The truth is, Charlene is one of these people who is a product of her surroundings and up-bringing. If she had just been encouraged to go to college, she would have discovered that she's actu-ally quite liberal, more intelligent than she thinks, and has an impeccable wit. Her observation skills are top-notch, and as a waitress - they aren't called servers here, they aren't libtards - she could people-watch all day long. She first started honing her imitation skills when she would make fun of some of the regulars to the rest of the staff. One of their most regular regulars was Don. Every morn-ing, he started his day with a cup of coffee and a fried egg, over easy, on toast at the diner. And so Charlene observed him the most over the years, and thus her imitation had ample opportunity to blossom.

"You're looking real pretty tonight, Don," Rayray said, pretending to swoon.

"Then you better tip big," she replied while pulling six bottles out of the cooler.

As she passed out the beers, Ralph addressed the group, "Seems Rayray was right."

"Good for you, babe," Charlene joked. But no one laughed.

Finishing a long swig, Rayray slammed his bottle down on the table. "Damn right," he said.

"What happened up there?" Charlene asked with concern.

"New neighbors," Ray answered.

Charlene hesitated for a moment before she asked, "Who?"

"Rami and Brooke," said Ralph. "Or that's who they say they are. Just bought the ranch up there and planning on moving in."

"They bought that whole ranch?" Charlene asked.

"That's what they said," Ralph said with a shrug.

An itch nagged at the back of Charlene's brain.

She pulled out her phone. "What were their names? Rami and…"

"Brooke," Rayray said as he looked over her shoulder.

The results of her Google search salved Charlene's itch. Her jaw dropped. "Oh my god. Do you know who they are?!" She was met with blank stares. "They're those people who got canceled last year!" The stares remained blank. "He was the CEO of that company - people thought she accused him of attempted rape or something…"

Rayray remembered, "Right. She's a reporter?"

Charlene digested and paraphrased her findings. "So he was CEO of DoggyBag… he gets fired because of the scandal… Whoa. He's worth, like, eight hundred million dollars!"

This raised the guys' suspicions further.

"Let's keep an eye on them," Ralph stated as he stood up and finished his beer before walking out.

The others nodded while Charlene imagined what you could do with that much money.

She'd soon find out.

Rami and Brooke retrieved their belongings from the farmhouse and began walking to the helicopter. The pilot started the engine, and the blades came to life.

"Are you worried?" Brooke asked, offering no opinion of her own in the delivery of the question.

"No," Rami said, surprising himself. The Rami of two years ago would be terrified and on the phone with his attorney this very instant to tell him to sell the property. But today's Rami had experienced rock bottom, and a group of beer-reeking locals didn't scare him.

"Good," Brooke said. And meant it. Which surprised her.

"But we should keep an eye on them," Rami said.

Brooke nodded.

Having reached the helicopter, they boarded and put on their headsets.

Brooke closed her eyes and leaned her head back as the vehicle began its fight with gravity.

I need to find a moving company, Rami thought as Brooke fell asleep beside him.

Chapter Seven

This one is just sad. I mean, they're all sad. Every one of them marks a life or lives destroyed by public opinion. But this one has so many layers of sadness to it that it's one I always hate to recount.

We're going to watch a news report that went viral so quickly that poor Dr. Hanover hadn't even had a chance to create a single social media account before all of social media had already canceled him.

This is a report from a news station in Boston.

Tragedy struck off the coast of Massachusetts today when an amateur deep seadeep-sea fisher caught a locally beloved dolphin named Gloucester, resulting in the poor creature's painful death.

Named after the seaside town where locals first noticed and then rescued the poor dolphin,

Gloucester Glouster became a hero of sorts to children across the country when the story of his broken flipper and fight for survival went viral online. Unable to fight the current with only one working flipper and experiencing fatigue from exertion, Gloucester Glouster nevertheless never stopped trying to make it back to sea.

After being rescued, authorities took him to the Boston Aquarium, where he healed and quickly gained the adoration of children worldwide.

Crowds gathered this afternoon to watch Gloucester be released back into the wild, but the celebration was cut short only minutes after the dolphin was freed.

This is the worst part: they cut to footage that was recorded of the events.

The following footage may be too much for younger viewers at home.

That's Gloucester out in front. Ready yourself, the video is about to zoom in so you can see better.

You have a clear view of things as he makes a leap out of the water and executes a beautiful twist in mid-air.

And in just a moment, he dives…. and doesn't come back up. There's a scream; the camera pans over to violent thrashing in the water next to a deep sea fishing boat.

More people scream, and children begin crying as - yes, that is Gloucester's body being hauled out of the water.

Gloucester continues to thrash, and the fishing line goes slack, hurling him down and slamming his head into the side of the boat. The men on the boat are trying to release him - but when he starts to spray blood from his blowhole, they can't grip anything and keep falling and flailing.

Local authorities are investigating the incident; nothing is yet known about the boat's owner.

Rest In Peace, Gloucester, from all of us and our viewers at home.

To Brooke and Rami's relief, their move came with no drama, and they even started to get to know the locals.

Brooke's parents did not understand her reason for moving to Montana. They implored her not to throw away her career for a boy. Which is abso-lutely not what this is, but no matter how many times she corrected their misunderstanding of her and Rami's relationship, they still referred to him as "your boyfriend."

Rami's parents still refused to speak to him, so it didn't matter where he lived.

The standard, boring moving-in things transpired, though not without a few surprises. For instance, neither of them ever lived anywhere where you couldn't easily get internet. But - surprise, surprise - there isn't a convenient cable internet hookup way out in the middle of rural Montana.

The farmhouse hadn't been lived in for a few years, so there was plenty need for repairs. Over their first few weeks living there, Rami went on to hire many of the locals to do the work. When they concluded that the plumbing needed major work, they hired Derrick Hoover and Hoover & Sons. Derrick didn't have any sons. He was the son. He also didn't have a brother. But he did have three older sisters. The Hoover in Hoover & Sons had been his grandfather; the & Sons were his father and uncle. When Derrick's father took over the business, he decided it didn't make sense to re-name it Hoover & Daughters & Son. So he didn't.

Rami contracted Dickie for much of the work, and that's how Rami came to hire Dickie's buddy

Nando as an electrician. And because Nando knew how to charge high rates for his work while out-sourcing it to cheap labor, Willie and Wyatt did much of the work on the power lines and utility poles.

This experience would come in handy months later when they decided to take down all the power lines.

But that's still in the future. We don't need to worry about that now. Because Rami and Brooke are not worried about that. They will be. But not right now.

Right now, all Brooke and Rami are worried about is the snowstorm predicted to hit this week around Thanksgiving.

Charlene's brother, Frankie, was in town for the holiday.

Well, he will be in town for the holiday. He isn't in yet. Traffic from Bozeman is a nightmare right now due to an eighteen-wheeler and its con-tents strewn across all lanes of the highway in both directions.

He's still getting in at a good time. In fact, that time is in just a few seconds. Charlene has been cooking away alone while she waits for Frankie to arrive and Rayray to get home from a last-minute job.

Rayray, you see, is the best HVAC specialist in town. And when a storm's about to hit, there's always a job available. If he hadn't been offered triple his hourly rate, he wouldn't have taken the job on Thanksgiving day. But he and Charlene were saving up to have a baby soon, and every dollar was welcome.

And right on time: Frankie is knocking on the door to the garage.

Well, on time for me. He's about three hours late, according to Charlene. But that's because she didn't know that an eighteen-wheeler intended to dissect itself across Frankie's route to her house. If she had, she'd have been psychic. Which she isn't.

"Lenie?" Frankie called out as he opened the door to the garage. This is the door that family knows to use. It's an easy way for Charlene and Rayray to tell if it's someone they know or a stranger: strangers ring the front doorbell, friends and family know to enter through the garage.

"I'm in here!" she shouted back.

"In here" meant the kitchen just around the

corner. Frankie dropped his bag on the ground, where he had dropped it since he was nine.

That's how old Frankie was when he, Charlene, and their parents moved into this house. When their parents decided to move to Florida a couple of years ago, they offered to sell the house to Charlene and Rayray. It was a tiny point of contention between Charlene and Frankie. Frankie didn't want to move back to their hometown after college, so it's not like he really wanted the house. But at the same time, it felt kind of one-sided. Sure, Charlene and Rayray paid for their home; they weren't just gifted it. Like I said, it's a "tiny" point of contention. And truthfully, Frankie loved returning to his childhood home and putting his bag down where he always had. So he was glad that Charlene and Rayray had bought it so that it would stay in the family.

"Where's Rayray?" Frankie inquired after the typical welcoming hugs and small talk about how stupid traffic is.

"Oh, up at the old ranch again," she said, going back to the oven to check on the pies.

"What ranch?"

"You know. Who was it, the Holisters who used to own it? That old ranch."

"Someone finally bought it?"

"Not just someone," Charlene said with a smile that hinted at juicy gossip. And as a reporter for the Bozeman Daily Chronicle, he always kept his eyes and ears open for a juicy story. You'll be shocked to learn that not a whole lot of excitement happened in Bozeman. Or Montana in general. And so he didn't get to write on a great number of topics that interested him.

That would soon change, though.

"Who?" Frankie asked.

"Do you remember Rami Mahmoud?"

"No… Did we go to school with him?"

"From the news! It was like a year ago. And then the reporter who ruined his life got canceled a couple of months ago…"

"Wait. He bought the Holister's old farmhouse?"

"The whole ranch!"

Frankie ruminated on this for a moment. "Is he living there?"

"Not just him. That reporter too!"

This stunned Frankie silent. It was just too bizarre. Why did some Silicon Valley executive - or former executive - buy up that much property in Montana? "And Rayray is up there right now?"

"Wouldn't be if they hadn't offered to pay him triple."

This only piqued Frankie's curiosity more. While Charlene busied about the kitchen, he pulled out his phone and started to take down some notes.

Frankie most likely would have forgotten all about the note he jotted down once he saved it to his phone and put it in his pocket: out of sight, out of mind. He would not write a story about Rami and Brooke, so no article would be printed in the Bozeman Daily Chronicle, and Wille would not see the article and make her trek to the ranch. And this would be a very different story.

Instead - Rayray burst in through the door to the garage and shouted to whoever was home, "Looks like I'll need to head back up there after dinner."

And instead of saving his notes and forgetting about them, Frankie kept his notes open so he could jot down some more.

As Rayray got himself washed up and ready for dinner, Frankie followed him around the house, trying to extract every little bit of information from him. When Rayray finally ran out of answers, he offered to bring Frankie with him after dinner so he could meet them himself.

This effectively meant that Frankie landed the first interviews with Rami and Brooke post-cancelation.

Granted, neither Rami nor Brooke thought they were giving interviews. So neither looked up the Bozeman Daily Chronicle after meeting Frankie. And neither was even aware of the article until Willye and Wilson showed up on their doorstep some three weeks later.

We'll get to that. But first…

Unlike Charlene, Brooke is not busying herself about the kitchen cooking a Thanksgiving feast. Rami isn't either. They are too busy heating water up on the stove and then dumping it in the bathtub. It's the only way to get a hot bath when your boiler is busted.

Rami had been concerned Brooke would stay there for Thanksgiving so he wouldn't be lonely. So about two weeks ago, he broached the subject and asked if she needed a ride to the airport.

"I don't really celebrate the origin story of the decimation of my people," she replied.

And that was that. They'd stay in Montana and not celebrate Thanksgiving.

When Rayray and Frankie arrived, Rami was making fried rice. He hadn't learned how to cook, so Brooke started teaching him. "We'll start out with Dorm-Style Dining," she'd explained. Which basically meant: how to cook several meals with only a few ingredients and fewer cooking tools.

"Hope you don't mind," Rayray began as he took off his coat, "but I brought my brother-in-law with me, so he didn't get stuck washing the dishes."

"Frankie," Frankie offered with an extended hand. Rami shook it, and the usual pleasantries followed.

"Brooke is in the kitchen trying to fix whatever it is I made that is supposed to be fried rice," Rami explained as he took their coats.

"How do you like the place?" Frankie asked; a soft-ball question to get things started.

"I'll love it more when it's all fixed up, but it's a nice change from Chicago."

Rami immediately regretted mentioning Chicago.

Frankie immediately perked up. And Rami saw this. He couldn't tell if Frankie knew who he was, but he decided it didn't really matter.

"Why Montana?" Frankie asked.

Rami decided to just dive in head first: "I wanted to be somewhere nobody would know me," he said before quickly correcting himself, "We both were."

That's my in, thought Frankie.

"That's understandable after everything you two went through," he offered as an olive branch of sorts. Maybe a dash of empathy would get Rami to let down his guard even more.

Fortunately for Frankie, it had the desired effect.

Rami's guard down, he actually felt a bit of relief talking about this all with someone other than Brooke. None of the locals ever mentioned it, though he assumed they'd figured out who he and Brooke were by now.

Still unaware that Frankie was conducting an on-the-record interview, Rami answered his questions with complete candor. So much so that it sometimes took Frankie aback. Whenever Rami mentioned something of particular interest, Frankie had to find a moment to excuse himself to the bathroom so that he could quickly take down the note. He couldn't really have his phone out, tapping away on the screen in a fury while trying to capture every one of Rami's words with any discretion.

Frankie could happily stay for hours getting information out of Rami, but Rayray is an expert HVAC technician and finished up the work in about 20 minutes.

As Frankie and Rayray headed towards the door, Rami did something he never does and had, in fact, done only a few times in the past: he put his hand on Frankie's shoulder and said, "Really nice meeting you!" before shaking Frankie's hand one last time.

It would actually be the last time. Though Rami didn't know this in the moment. He would come to regret his attempt to make friends with Frankie. It embarrassed him for others to see his gullibility. But mostly, he just felt lonely when the article came out and learned that Frankie's friendliness had been a facade. It was a reminder that not only did he only have a single friend, but it would be an uphill battle to make new friends.

Ironically, making new friends would soon be the least of Rami's worries. In just a few months, he'd have too many people who wanted to be his friend and who considered him theirs.

And, perhaps as is fitting, it was, in fact, Frankie's article that would bring these new friends Rami's way.

I'm not sure how long the others were at Don's before Rayray and Frankie showed up. I was too busy following the goings on at the Ranch when one of the guys, probably Dickie, buzzed Don's doorbell after Thanksgiving dinner and got him to open up.

Don's doorbell rang upstairs in the apartment he lived in above the bar - and he only answered it late at night if you knew the secret buzz: hold for 2 seconds, wait 1 second, then two quick, staccato buzzes.

So whoever buzzed him that evening knew the secret buzz. Which isn't a huge surprise.

Everyone in town knows the secret buzz.

When Rayray and Frankie left the ranch,

Rayray instinctively drove to Don's without much thought. Fortunately, Don's was, in fact, open. But if it hadn't been, he knew the secret buzz.

They walked into a room full of men sloppy on tryptophan and beer who definitely should not be driving home tonight. But would be. And only after "just one more."

Gerry was the only one not drinking. His dad had a drinking problem, and he never found much joy in it. So he was the one doing most of the talking while everyone else listened.

"I'm telling you, all those deliveries to the ranch are doing wonders for business. None of those drivers want to run out of gas on their way back, and most of them are picking up at least a coffee or something." Gerry is the one who works at the gas station and is the first in town to meet Willye and Wilson. This meeting is not too far in his future, so this evening's conversation will be fresh in his mind when the two walk in.

"That's how they first sedate you, Gerry," Rayray began, "by making you love their presence. It's what every major corporation does when they move some distribution center into a community." Rayray hung his coat on the back of an empty chair. Frankie grew up with everyone, so he said his own hellos and how've-you-beens but kept an ear on what Rayray was saying.

Frankie admired Rayray. While Rayray still lived and worked in their hometown and Frankie moved to the city, he never felt like Rayray settled, and in some ways, still considered Rayray more successful than he and so someone to admire.

"Rayray, you're making some good money working on that farmhouse of theirs," Gerry said in an attempt to one-up Rayray. But, of course, no one in this room was better read than Rayray, and no one ever won an argument with him.

"Yes, I am. And you know what goes through my head? What happens when he needs more work done than I can handle?" No one spoke. No one had a good answer. No one even had a particularly good guess. Though that didn't stop Bart from saying, "You hire me?" Rayray thought that Bart was being a smart ass and lashed out, "You'd quit after you broke a nail."

Bart turned hot and blushed. The familiar paranoia crept in. Rayray only knew that barb would sink deep because he grew up making fun of how Bart had lady fingers and not man hands. Worse,

Rayray caught Bart nursing a broken nail once in the 6th grade. So to bring this up meant Rayray was digging deep to wound him with knowledge that only came to those who observed another closely with suspicion.

Who else has seen me do something and is holding onto it for just the right moment? he wondered. This depressed him. A common state of mind for Bart lately. He remained silent the rest of the night.

Even though his question was heartfelt. He'd always hoped he could work for Rayray someday.

See, Rayray is one of these people who can be so nice and friendly when he's in public and so nasty in private.

Rayray felt the air grow heavy. He'd embarrassed the room by airing something between brothers in front of their friends. He wanted to apologize. But that isn't something he is capable of yet. So he drove attention back to the original topic.

"What happens, Gerry, when there's enough business driving through here that a BP decides to open up?" Rayray threw out to the group. This did a fantastic job of distracting everyone from the awkwardness of the last 90 seconds, as no one had thought about something like that. Which makes sense, as none of them were Rayray.

Gerry remained silent. He had no retort.

But Ralph did: "Then why are you taking their money?" he asked without looking up from his beer.

Rayray's ears burned. Tonight's apparently the night of brothers hurling barbs at each other. "You know why," was all Rayray said. All he had to say.

The why is because in vitro fertilization is expensive. But it's the only way he and Charlene can get pregnant.

"Any worry about others moving to town?" Frankie asked to cut the tension.

"Why would anyone else want to move here?" Ray asked. He, again, had been sitting silently, listening.

"I don't know. Because they're tired of city living and want to get away from it all? And some nice millionaire has already paved the way for them? Literally?"

The room took this in. It was a completely new thought.

"They'd have to..." Dickie began before realizing

he didn't know how the idea ended. No one had any ideas for how to end it.

"They'd have to buy up some land and develop it," Rayray pointed out. "Which they could do. Or a bank could buy up land, break it up into plots, and turn it into a gated community. Or…"

"So we're fucked," Ralph summarized.

"No, I'm just saying… we shouldn't let our guard down," Rayray explained, "We don't know them. They don't know us. They have no reason to consider our wishes in any of their decision-making."

"Then we'll need to look after our own interests," Ralph said.

The others nodded.

Frankie tapped away on his phone wildly.

This was the story that would make his name as a journalist.

❖

The story didn't make Frankie's name as a journalist.

In fact, he considered it a complete and utter failure.

Not only did it have the lowest views of any story that week, but it also received the lowest views of any story in the past sixteen months. The story from sixteen months ago that performed worse than his boringed-people-to-death about how a growing shortage of cheese powder put the entire instant macaroni and cheese industry at risk.

One of the people who read it was Randle, who worked over at the diner with Charlene. That poor idiot went and spent all of his savings stocking up on instant macaroni and cheese. He didn't even like the stuff so much as he thought it would be worth a lot of money someday when the powdered cheese supply in the US dried up. Randle is not someone you want in charge of investing your money.

Randle did not read Frankie's story.

No one from that night at Don's read the story.

No one from town read the story.

But!

The Shepherd Express picked up the story in Milwaukee as a sort of News of the Weird column.

The article from the Shepherd Express then popped up in the news feed of a young man named Wilson, age 12, while he scrolled on social media - as he often did, seeing as he had no friends.

His grandmother, Willye, age mind-your-own-business, sitting next to him knitting, glanced over and caught the headline:

Canceled Couple Seeks Refuge in Montana Wilderness

At that moment, she didn't know what compelled her to take the tablet out of Wilson's hands and tap on the article. Later, she would say that it must have been the gentle urging of God that she reached down and took hold of their future. Willye, you see, grew up religious and remained that way since. Wilson was starting to question the teachings of the Bible but was not yet an angst-ridden enough teenager to start yelling at her about hypocrisies and shellfish.

Her belief system, however, did not prevent her from joining the technology revolution. As she liked to joke to her friends - well, former friends - she was "one of those tech-savvy grannies."

She didn't make that joke anymore. She hadn't in a while.

She had no friends to joke with.

She soon would, though, and they would meet mere days after she and Wilson arrived at Rami and Brooke's doorstep.

That future friend was none other than Dr. Gene Hanover, who would see the article two days later, sitting alone in his family medical practice office in Newburyport, MA. The Eagle-Tribune, his local paper, had also picked it up as a News of the Weird column.

When Rami learns how Willye, Wilson, and Dr. Hanover came to learn about him and Brooke in Montana, he will be genuinely embarrassed that his story is considered weird enough to laugh at. But that's for later.

When the story of the beloved dolphin, Gloucester, dying at his hands in such a messy, horrific way went viral, his patients stopped coming by, like a water faucet turned off at the source. The harassing phone calls to his office were so bad that his staff quit within days of the news. Even his sister, his receptionist for over 20 years, resigned.

But he diligently went to work each day, "just in case someone needs me." The old doctor dedicated his life to the Hippocratic oath, and not being needed devastated him.

So when he read a story about two social outcasts, much like himself, finding a place to live amongst people again, his heart skipped a beat. He had not had a real conversation with someone in over eight months.

Willye and Wilson had been living on the social tundra of the world for over a year. He tried to return to school immediately after the incident with the ball, but the ridicule and harassment were too much. Worse, it brought a new round of attention to his public shame. And a few months after that, when opening day came, they started the first game by having the seat he'd been sitting in removed "because it was cursed" - the press descended upon him yet again to see if he wanted to comment.

Eventually, Willye pulled him from school and tried to put him in a private school. But none were willing to take someone, no matter how gifted, who might draw unwanted attention to the school and its other students and faculty.

So homeschooling it was. Which was not what Willye wanted for Wilson. But her only options seemed to be either Wilson suffering through the neverending cycles of public shaming that appeared to come with every major milestone that could be tied to that incident or removing him from the public eye and not providing any more fuel for their superstitious pyre. At some point, they have to get bored with that stupid ball, she thought to herself as her mind danced with the idea of going out to Montana to see these folks in the article. But until they get bored with that damn ball, maybe we can find some solace with these two.

A doctor's always handy to have around, Dr. Hanover thought to himself as he read the article.

And Wilson thought, When is she going to be done...

"I'll be done when I'm done," Willye said, not moving or looking at him in any way.

His jaw dropped.

"That's right. I can read minds," she said with a smile.

And Wilson believed her.

As he should.

Grandmothers can read minds.

It was probably a week after Frankie's article ran in the Bozeman Daily Chronicle that Bart was driving past the gas station where Gerry worked and decided he needed a fill-up.

He didn't need a fill-up. He had plenty of gas to run his few errands.

But for some reason, any time he saw Gerry's new mechanic, Ron, working in the garage, he felt compelled to stop by, whether he had a reason or not.

Tonight, he did not. But when he got out of his truck, he saw Ron standing inside the store rather than working in the garage. He didn't recognize Ron at first because he was wearing a flannel shirt. Ron usually worked in an old t-shirt.

So instead of chatting with Ron outside the garage while he filled up his tank, he changed his mind about needing gas and realized instead that what he really needed was a cup of coffee and maybe something else.

As he walked in, he did not take notice of the car with Wisconsin license plates pulling into the spot next to his truck. He did take notice of the jeans Ron was wearing, which weren't covered in oil stains.

Manifesting his most casual walk possible, Bart made his way to the coffee station. Fortune was on his side this day, as Ron was also getting coffee.

While striking up a mundane conversation

with Ron, Bart did not hear the doorbell chime as two strangers walked in.

He eventually looked up and saw the reflection of Gerry - expressing some expression of dismay - trying to make eye contact with him in the security mirror. Bart at first feared that Gerry saw him do something that made him think Bart was doing something he shouldn't be doing. He lowered his eyes in shame for a moment before realizing that hiding would make him look more guilty, so he looked back up at the security mirror quickly.

Gerry gestured with his head while Bart didn't hear the cooler right behind him open up and close. He shrugged, mouthing "What?" back at Gerry.

And then he found out what: as an elderly Black woman said, "Excuse me," from over his shoulder. He stepped aside to see her and a young boy walk up to the register.

Chapter Eight

Brooke was tiling the bathroom. She's one of those people who have the patience and endurance to tile a bathroom. If you haven't ever tried, you're lucky. If you have, you know what I mean.

Rami offered to hire a contractor to do the work, but she already felt like she was mooching off him. So she found ways to contribute that helped alleviate her guilt. And tiling was one way she could contribute.

Besides, if contractors did all of the work, it wouldn't be a home; it would be a diorama. Little imperfections at the hands of the home's residents were beauty marks in her mind. Perfection unnerved her. She spent much too much of her life chasing perfection, only to be taught every single time that the blonde girl would always be seen as more perfect. She considered attaining ideal beauty, or perfection in general, to be cowardice parading as happiness.

While wiping stray grout off a piece of blue tile, she heard a car pulling up the driveway.

The car was unexpected. Rami was home. Where else would he be? she thought. And it didn't sound like one of the locals' trucks - which always sound like one of the locals' trucks because they loved that people could hear them before seeing them.

Brooke was not frightened, but she was cautious. Growing up in Chicago, she learned self-defense and how to use a gun. Which is why she owned a gun. And why she withdrew one from her purse sitting on the front room couch. She kept the safety on - no need to assume this is anything other than a purely precautionary measure. But she sure kept her finger on that little button so she could flick it off in an instant if necessary.

"Rami?" she called out, keeping her eyes on the driveway. He didn't answer. She pulled her phone out of her pocket and turned down the music she was listening to while working. She could hear Rami in the upstairs shower.

She took a deep breath and opened the front door. As she watched the car pull up about 100 feet from the porch, she flicked on the porch and driveway lights.

The Subaru caught in the bright light was not what Brooke expected to see. Not that she expected anything in particular. She is not a gearhead who recognizes the tones and harmonics of car engines and can recall the make, model, and year just from the sound of it.

The first door to open was not the driver's door but the one behind it.

Out leaped a young boy who did a sort of hoppy dance up the stairs to her and asked, "Where's the bathroom?" with urgency clenching his voice.

Brooke, who did not typically let complete strangers into her house, found herself letting a complete stranger into her house. "Down and to the right," she said, though she shouted the latter half as the kid whizzed down the hallway, trying not to whiz down his pants.

As the older woman approached the steps, Brooke heard clanging and ripping, followed by a painful-sounding thud, erupting from the bathroom. Rami! she realized. "Hold on!" Brooke shouted to Willye.

"Brooke!?" came the muffled shout of Rami.

"Hold on!" Brooke shouted to the bathroom audience. She quickly turned back to the old woman and said, without shouting, "Hold on a moment, please," before darting back into the house.

She arrived at the bathroom door to a scene featuring a young boy, maybe a teenager - he was tall - zipping up his fly while a sea creature writhed under the shower curtain and curtain rod.

"Is someone in here with me?!" Rami asked mid-thrash.

"Sorry! I couldn't hold it any longer!" said the child with a man's deep voice.

Brooke halted for a second, taken aback by the voice. The child ran out the door shouting, "Sorry!" behind him.

"Brooke!" Rami cried out.

She yanked the towel off the back of the bathroom door. She grabbed part of the shower curtain, turned her head away, and pulled while thrusting the towel forward with her other hand. When she felt the towel ripped out of her hand, she waited another few seconds before turning back to him.

Too bad, Brooke thought as she caught her first glimpse of Rami in nothing but a towel. Cleaning out the barn put some nice muscle on Rami's frame. Of course, her lot in life would be to live with an attractive man who didn't want to touch her. She rolled her eyes for no one but herself.

"Who's that?" Rami asked, pushing a towel around the floor with his foot to soak up the water he'd splashed all over the place.

"I have no idea," Brooke said as she grabbed another towel to help him.

He stopped. "What do you mean?"

"I hope we didn't…" the voice from the door began, causing both Brooke and Rami to scream. Rami slipped on a puddle he hadn't wiped up and tumbled to the floor.

"… scare you," the old woman finished.

"Not at all!" Brooke assured her, despite Rami having to hoist himself back off the floor again.

"Why don't I let you two…" Willye began.

"You're so fine!" Brooke shouted at the same time Rami said, "That would be much appreciated."

Willye didn't finish her sentence. Instead, she turned around and went back to the porch.

She walked over to where Wilson sat on the porch stairs. He leaned his head on her leg. "Are we staying?"

"Yes, we are," Willye said with complete confidence.

"They said we can stay?!" Wilson asked, surprised to hear that everything was already settled.

"No, not yet," she replied without concern.

"Then how do you know?"

"I read minds, remember?"

The meal was nothing fancy. Beef stew and baked-from-frozen dinner rolls.

Willye and Wilson were not offended. They were hungry and appreciative of the generosity. Something they had not experienced in too long.

While Rami had been drying off and getting dressed, Brooke returned to the porch and invited Willye and Wilson in. Happy to have friendly company other than Rami, Brooke asked if they'd like to stay for dinner.

Wilson gave his grandmother a worried look as the offer didn't seem to come with accommodations. She winked at him with a smile and thanked Brooke for the offer.

All four seated around the kitchen table, the sound of clinking spoons against the sides of bowls was all the conversation taking place. No one really knew how to start the conversation. Finally, Rami started with something simple: "So where are you from?"

"We're from Wisconsin, just outside Milwaukee," Willye explained.

"We're practically neighbors," Brooke joked. "Were. Were practically neighbors," she corrected herself.

"Well, about that..." Willye started. Then she stopped. She actually prepared her request prior to departing Wisconsin as improvisation never revealed itself as one of her strengths. This was not a situation where she wanted to wing it.

"Our intention, driving out here, was to ask if we could stay here with you," she said. This took both Brooke and Rami by complete surprise, and neither knew how to respond.

At last, Rami came up with a question: "Why?"

"Our lives are ruined, the same as yours," she replied. "His more so."

The two looked at Wilson. He had stopped playing with his tablet but still kept his eyes on the screen.

Neither Brooke nor Rami ever claimed to be baseball fans, but the story of Wilson's Ball lived on the periphery of their pop culture knowledge. Neither, however, knew anything about Wilson's life after that fateful catch. Willye, not wanting to make Wilson relive the past year and a half, told the boy he could be excused and go play with his tablet.

Here comes a moment that is yet another example of why I love Brooke:

As Willye recounts the story and reaches the part where Wilson is humiliated in the boys' bathroom at school, Brooke's heart breaks.

Her own Middle School torment resurfaces from the deep well of dark memories we all have, and all have pushed down until we forgot about them. She feels for this boy she doesn't know at all. Because in at least one way - this way - she knows him.

Brooke's empathy is boundless, sometimes to her detriment. But she would never trade it away to be a more guarded person who is hurt less.

That's why I love her. She chooses to be vulnerable, knowing full well and good that she's destined to be hurt again at some point in the - probably very near - future.

Which is why she wanted to say yes to their request without hesitation, while Rami wanted to think it over. He explained that the other five bedrooms in the house didn't come with any furniture, so they couldn't offer them beds. But they were welcome to sleep on the couches downstairs if that was okay.

"This will be just fine, thank you," Willye said with a groan as she sat down in a recliner. "I spent many nights sleeping next to my husband in our recliners after he got sick and couldn't lay down comfortably anymore." She turned to Wilson, "Do you mind the couch?"

"Better than the backseat," he said and yawned. The mere suggestion of sleep made his eyelids feel heavy. He plopped down on one of the couches, but it was about two inches too short for him to lay out flat. He had to put his feet up on the armrest, which wasn't all that comfortable. So he moved to the other couch where he could stretch out uninhibited.

His grandmother watched this series of events and said to herself, "Boy's getting taller every day."

As they neared Rami's bedroom, Brooke took ahold of his shirt sleeve and tugged on it, signaling for him to follow her.

So he did.

Upstairs and to her bedroom door.

"You're going to let them, right?" she asked as soon as she figured they were out of earshot.

Rami didn't answer. He was still thinking about it.

"What are the reasons for not letting them stay?"

"I can think of plenty," he retorted.

"How many are worse than what that kid's been through?"

Rami couldn't think of any. All he could do was stand there and nod. *That is the question, isn't it?* he thought.

He smiled at Brooke, turned, and headed downstairs to his bedroom.

While it didn't seem like the job would be anything worth talking about, Ralph sure was heading back to town with a lot to talk about.

Rami hadn't decided yet whether Willye and Wilson were staying, but he was considering it enough that he decided to have the downstairs rooms reinsulated. When he was the only one living on the first floor, he didn't mind the draftiness of the downstairs bedrooms. But now that three of them lived on that floor - maybe three of them - it seemed like the right time to get the work done.

When he asked Rayray who he recommended for the job, Rayray suggested Ralph without hesitation. "Been doing it for years. Does the job quick. In and out," Rayray told Rami.

As you know, Ralph knew of Willye and Wilson's presence on the property. Bart made sure of that. And even though Bart didn't remember the detail about the two of them maybe moving to the ranch, Gerry did and made sure to tell Ralph and the boys about it the next time he visited Don's. Which just happened to be later that very same night.

Ralph didn't enjoy detective work, so he didn't plan to pry for information or look for clues. But he would keep his ears and eyes open while he installed the insulation. And that's how he heard confirmation that the new two were staying.

Brooke waited until Willye and Wilson left for a walk around the property to ask Rami if he planned to let them stay. "You're insulating their rooms," she started before he cut her off with, "They're not their rooms yet!"

"Yet!"

"Why are you so sure?" he asked, taking her by surprise. He hadn't asked before.

"I know what he's gone through."

"And that means it's a good idea for him to live here? There aren't any other kids."

"I think that's the point."

"Is that healthy?" he asked, growing exasperated.

"I don't think that's for us to decide," she reminded him.

"Fine. But long-term…" he began.

"Long-term, Rami, is a big fucking question mark. For all of us."

Ralph became conscious of the silence hanging in the air, indicating he wasn't moving and, thus, most likely eavesdropping. So he quickly went back to work.

"I'm here because I don't know what comes next," she said. "I think they are too. This is our hiding place for now. Who knows for how long. But for now, it's what I need. It's what you need. It's what they need."

Rami nodded. "You're right."

Ralph didn't overhear Rami asking Willye and Wilson if they wanted to move in, but he knew the moment it happened based on the "Praise the lord!" he heard coming from the front porch.

"It's official!"

Those were the first words out of Ralph's mouth after he burst in through Rayray and Charlene's front door.

"They're staying!" he said, taking off his hat and throwing it down on the couch before picking it up and sitting there instead. I get it. What did that hat do to deserve a seat?

Charlene's first thought wasn't *Wwho* the they *They* who were staying were. It was, It's been a while.

What it had been a while since was Ralph's last bursting in.

Bursting in became a common occurrence after JuliEtta's death when Ralph hit his mental and emotional low point. Sometimes he would be in the middle of something - shaving, grocery shopping, mowing the lawn - and he'd just drop what he was doing and go over to their house. It seemed to Charlene like the will to live had been sucked out of him, and he needed to be convinced to give it another go.

When JuliEtta died, her brother Rayray took it the hardest since they were close enough in age to be friends, but she was young enough for him to feel protective.

She also happened to be the person who got Rayray into reading. His love of reading wasn't innate - it was born from a desire to do anything to make his little sister happy.

Here's a funny insight into the Mulfords: they did suspect one of their sons might be gay but actually never suspected Bart. It was Rayray who worried them up until he met Charlene.

Rayray, you see, could better mother JuliEtta than their own mother. He made sure that her laundry got washed, he set out her clothes for the next school day, he made her lunch for her - which made her the only Mulford kid to ever bring a lunch to school - and generally doted on her from the moment his parents brought her home from the hospital until the moment Ralph became her husband.

It probably won't surprise you, then, that Charlene and JuliEtta grew up "best friends forever." In some ways, Rayray had been jealous of Charlene when they were growing up because she got more of JuliEtta's attention than he did. But that changed after puberty struck and Charlene's breasts showed up at school one day.

Over the next couple of years, Charlene changed from the twig of a kid always hanging around his sister to the full-bodied woman Rayray didn't know he would one day find attractive. Rayray's mother had been a strong woman with meat on her bones, and the more Charlene's body took on these qualities, the more Rayray thought about her.

Rayray was respectful, though, and never made any moves on Charlene or asked her out to any dances or nights at the movies. He didn't want to put Charlene and JuliEtta's friendship at risk.

Which is why it was actually JuliEtta who convinced Rayray to ask Charlene out.

So when JuliEtta passed, the three who hurt the most were the two currently seated and listening to the ramblings of the one standing and currently rambling.

And it was only because he burst in rambling, which he had done so often in the recent past but not at all in the last few months, that they remained seated and did not try to calm him down with the offer of a beer.

"Ralph, what are you talking about, buddy?" Rayray asked.

"The old woman and her, her… whatever he is to her!"

"Willye and Wilson?" Charlene asked.

Rayray and Ralph both looked at her.

"The grandmother and her grandson. Willye and Wilson." Charlene got no reaction or response from the guys. "Hello?" she joked, sort of.

"How do you know their names?" Ralph asked, each word coming slower than the last.

"They came in and ate at the dinner yesterday," she said with a shrug.

Rayray and Ralph looked at each other.

"Did they tell you anything about their… plans?" Rayray inquired.

"I asked if he was going to go to school with the kids around here, and she said no. Um… we mostly talked about how it's a big change from Milwaukee."

Rayray tensed up at the mention of Milwaukee. He didn't really know their story all that much, so he couldn't remember if he knew they lived in Milwaukee. But even if he didn't know before - he knew now. And this factoid set a mental Rube Goldberg device in motion, whirring and clacking and pinging around Rayray's brain. He is unaware of this, mind you, as it takes place entirely in the background at the hands of his well-read subconscious. But he feels something brewing. A thought is being formed. It was just an itch right now, but that's also because one last piece of the machine had not been set into motion.

That piece was dressed all in white and would arrive in less than two hours.

"Did they tell you anything else?" Ralph urged Charlene.

"I'm sure they did, but Randle was off, so I was running the place by myself. I didn't really have time to entertain, Ralph."

"Okay, okay, that's not what he's saying, Lenie," Rayray said, trying to de-escalate the situation. He blushed a bit, realizing that Ralph just heard him call her by her childhood nickname, which he still called her by when they were alone.

"I don't know why you're so paranoid," she spat at Ralph.

"Because I've been to Chicago. I've been to Milwaukee. To Minneapolis. Cleveland. Boston. Memphis. Atlanta." He caught himself getting emotional. Charlene felt ashamed; she'd forgotten how much Ralph hated the "city elite" after how he and JuliEtta were treated. Cold, unfazed, walking medical degrees with no desire to know their patients or extend empathy. No community. Just insurance claims and rapid discharges. "These are not good people," Ralph concluded after taking a few seconds to stabilize his emotional state.

Charlene lost the desire to argue, and Rayray was too distracted with worry for Ralph to keep his mind on the thought that was coming.

"I need a drink," Rayray said, not because he needed one, but because he knew Ralph needed one.

"I'll join you," Ralph said. "Sorry about my bursting in, Charlene," Ralph started.

"You're always welcome, Ralph," she assured him, "You know that."

He nodded.

He did know that.

Rayray and Charlene were the closest he had to family anymore.

"I wish JuliEtta…" Ralph started to say before turning around and heading back to his truck without another word.

Rayray and Charlene stood there watching him walk away. It killed them every time he started to talk about her. It's the most vulnerable you'll ever see Ralph Elmore.

Then Rayray put his arm around Charlene, kissed her on the top of her head, and gave her a squeeze.

"Don't wait up," he said.

I never do, she thought.

❖

Truer words could not be said, thought Ralph after saying these exact words to Rayray: "It's just like you said."

The reason Ralph said, "It's just like you said," was because he was saying it to Rayray, who had said that the end of "their world" would first come in the form of people from cities moving to Montana and communities like theirs.

This was triggered by what Ron said after he entered Don's and right before he gave Bart an erection.

The erection was the product of Ron patting Bart's thigh as he glided past him. Bart was somewhat confused by his body's reaction but didn't spend too much time thinking about it because Ralph was in the middle of saying, "It's just like you said." And to tell the truth, Bart had been so busy looking at how tight Ron's sleeves hugged the muscles in his shoulders and arms that he missed what Ron was saying as he walked toward him.

This is what Ron was saying as Bart walked toward him: "Who's the guy from Boston?"

Now, to understand why Ron would say such a thing, you'd have to go back about a minute to when he was getting out of his truck, and Doc Hanover was walking back to his Volvo.

Ron noticed the Massachusetts license plates on the Doc's car. He then asked the question always asked when someone finds out you're from Massachusetts: "You from Boston?"

The Doc just wanted to get out of there, so he did what most people from Massachusetts do when asked if they are from Boston: he said, "Yep!"

Most people from Massachusetts who confirm that they are from Boston are not from Boston. But it's a trap to say, "No, I'm actually from Newburyport," because then you have to explain where that is in relation to Boston, which then leads to more questions and probably some tales about how they wish they lived by the ocean, that's where they want to retire someday - the ocean.

Doc smiled and got into his car, paranoid that Ron may have recognized him. Had he revealed too much?

He put his phone back on the magnetic holder attached to his windshield and took a breath.

Here we go, he thought as he put the car into reverse.

As the Doc pulled back onto the main road, Ron entered Don's and kicked off the series of events leading to Bart hiding an erection while Ralph said, "It's just like you said."

"Chicago, Milwaukee, Boston. This is just the beginning," Rayray confirmed. "We'll see more of these folks coming in from cities and outnumbering those of us who are native to this land."

Rayray did not see the irony in calling the locals "native" to this land. Nor did he think about how it was fitting for them to be scared about losing what had been theirs for generations when that was the way their past generations had acquired said land from the actual natives in the first place.

"It's, what, just five of them up there. And that's if whoever-that-was ends up staying," said Gerry.

"It doesn't happen overnight, Gerry," Rayray shot back.

"We must be vigilant," Ralph chimed in, quoting Rayray from a past conversation. Rayray nodded with pride.

"So what do we do?" Bart asked, his erection fully deflated.

"We keep an eye on them," Ralph said.

Doc Hanover drove on some dangerous and dark roads in his day. New England is rife with treacherous terrain camouflaged as natural beauty. There are few places where you can plunge to your death while admiring the foliage.

But this drive unnerved him. While he didn't think going over a cliff seemed very likely, he was in unfamiliar territory and hadn't been for a very long time.

The good doctor, you see, spent his entire life in New England.

Sure, he went on vacations and traveled to other parts of the US - but he never left the North American continent. Montreal is the most exotic destination he has ever visited.

He turned on the radio to pass the time. He knew that radio was out of style or something like that. But he still loved it. He always played the radio in his waiting and visitation rooms, usually some classic station. It's one of the things about his practice that makes him feel so comfortable and old-fashioned to his patients.

Well, used to. Now there were no patients. And not much reason to play the radio.

He turned the radio off.

The silence sat uncomfortably with him, though, and soon he said out loud for no one to hear, "The hell with it!" and turned the radio up full blast.

Driving down the dirt road at night, he wound the window down and felt the cool breeze.

He thought of Mona. His wife of forty-two years. Gone the past three Thanksgivings.

They used to take drives like this on the

weekends. The picture in his mind is still crystal clear: Mona, passenger window down, leaning out, smiling at the side view mirror as she watches the world fly behind her. She hears an Elvis tune start on the radio and quickly turns it up. The scarf on her head starts to blow away. She catches it with one hand, flat on her head, laughing her ebullient laugh.

He turned the radio off again.

It had been sudden. Unexpected. Some even called it a freak accident.

It took days for the police to figure out how she died.

Her own car ran her over.

She never saw it coming.

Which somewhat comforted Gene. He couldn't stand the thought that fear was the last thing she experienced before dying. If she had to die without him by her side, let it have happened so quickly that she didn't know she was dying, let alone alone.

Here's the thing: he would never have bought that deep sea fishing boat and gone on that fateful trip if Mona was still alive.

Mona spent her whole life as a working

professional. She still did law work on the side even though she retired recently. Something uncommon about Mona and Gene is that Mona was ten years his senior.

Gene knew she had her own life insurance policy. But he never imagined she would leave him with so much set aside.

When the paperwork arrived and he saw the sum that would be deposited into their joint checking account - he hadn't taken her name off of it yet - he was gobsmacked. What followed next, however, was immense guilt. That momentary feeling of excitement had betrayed decades of a life he built with the woman he loved.

It was blood money. Nothing more.

And without Mona, there was little he could spend it on to bring himself happiness. So he decided to spend it on risk-taking. Best case scenario, Mona's money would lead to their reunification in the afterlife.

Worst case scenario, he'd impulsively purchase a deep sea fishing vessel, hire an amateur crew, and then proceed to massacre, in bright crimson, the most beloved sea mammal on the northern seaboard.

Who knew that the worst-case scenario was what he'd be dealt?

He could see the lights at the gate rising over the horizon.

Am I really doing this? he thought to himself. Then after a few seconds, he replied out loud, "Who fucking cares!"

He blushed. He couldn't remember the last time he said the word fuck.

It felt so good.

He turned the radio back on and sang along with the Billy Joel song playing.

Falling prey to the hypnotism of roads at night paired with familiar melodies, the rest of the drive blinked by for the Doctor. Somehow, he was already at the gate to the property. It was open. Not necessarily inviting, but definitely not threatening the prompt execution of trespassers.

When he pulled up to the house, he was surprised by the number of cars.

He was more surprised, however, by the child sitting on the front stairs. I didn't know he had a kid - or she had a kid, he thought inaccurately about Rami and Brooke. "Ma!" the boy shouted behind him, not taking his eyes off his tablet.

His next surprise was when Willye opened the door to the front porch and looked him up and down. "Can I help you?" she asked.

"Um… Mrs. Mahmoud?" Doc Hanover asked. This sent Willye into wild laughter.

Things were not proceeding as the doctor anticipated, and he even doubted if he was at the right property for a moment. He was about to get back into his car when Brooke came out to see what had Willye cackling.

"Brooke?!" he asked upon seeing her.

"Yes?" she responded with guarded hesitation.

"I'm Doctor Hanover!" He paused. Then realized that meant nothing to them. "Um, I'm - I mean, I'm Gene Hanover."

"Oh, I think you must have the wrong…" address was what she was about to say when he interrupted her: "I'm the Dolphin, uh…" He took a breath. "I'm Doctor Dolphin Death," he said with shame.

"You're… oh my god. You are!" The second the words left Brooke's mouth, it hit her why he was there. "You read the article?" He nodded. "Then I guess you should come on in," she said before shouting, "Rami!" into the house.

Walking inside, the neat, if conservative, interior surprised Doc Hanover. He expected something a little more rundown. Don't worry. His expectations will be met when he discovers that his bedroom has a leak in the ceiling. But since he didn't live here these past few weeks, he never witnessed the work that went into this place and couldn't fully appreciate how much of a transformation the house really experienced.

Willye opened the coat closet near the front door and held out a coat hanger to the doctor. He took off his blazer and hung it in the closet. "We're a casual household," she told him and then walked on by into the living room.

Following behind her, Gene asked, "So, do you know Rami or Brooke?"

"Both, I guess," she said, "though neither really."

"You saw the article?"

"Mm hm. And came to the same conclusion as you, it would seem."

He looked down at the suitcases he was carrying. "Ah, yes. A bit presumptuous of me, I suppose."

She shrugged and sat down on one of the couches.

Brooke returned with Rami in tow. She gave him a quick rundown of Doc Hanover's infamy as they walked down the hallway. Rami knew none of this story and was just hearing about the gushing gore when he turned the corner and almost walked into the doctor himself. "Ah, you must be Doctor…"

"Gene Hanover. Mr. Mahmoud?" Doc Hanover asked with as much humility as possible. Which had the singular effect of making Rami's stomach churn. He always felt significant discomfort whenever someone much older than him deigned to him. It felt awful when old white investors did it to him at DoggyBag, and it felt awful now.

"Rami, please," Rami corrected him. "Really. Please. Just Rami."

"Rami," the doctor said. He said this because it's something we do when we want someone to think we are listening to them: we repeat back the last thing they said.

"Have a seat," Rami offered before sitting next to Willye. Doc Hanover took a seat in the chair nearest him. To describe the experience of sitting in it as uncomfortable would be too nice. But the doctor did not intend to complain and ask for a better seat. To be amongst people who did not look at him with curiosity or disdain, who treated him like he remembered being treated, thrilled him. He accepted the uncomfortable chair as a small expense for the pleasure of this company.

"You have no idea how long it's been since someone said that to me," Doc Hanover said; he sounded melancholic yet hopeful.

"I'm sure we all do," Rami reminded him.

"True," the doctor said. And then silence followed. They were waiting for him to say something. So he said, "Thank you for inviting me in. It's been a long drive."

"State your business," Willye said, looking over her glasses at him.

"Well, I think it's probably similar to yours," he said. "I lost... everything that matters. My wife died a few years ago, and that was bad enough. But then the shaming..." He stopped. Then he looked right into Willye's eyes and said, "You know, I really did consider... ending it. When you've lived this long and don't have much left to live for, you have to wonder if you're just taking up space and resources that could better serve someone else.

You're lucky you have your grandson to give you purpose."

"To tell the truth, even purpose wasn't enough on some days to keep the same thought from creeping into my head," she said, putting her hand on his knee. "I know that's a terrible thing to say. But there were days in those first few weeks that I couldn't imagine going on. Either of us. I couldn't imagine his future without torment." She sat back. "So you want to move in," she said for him.

"I'm sure I can be of use. I may be old, but I'm not done yet. And I'm a practicing physician. I'm not asking to move in forever. Just to live, for a little bit, like I used to. Just some distance from the public gaze."

Rami considered this. He knew what Brooke would do. But this wasn't exactly what he had in mind when he bought the property. Well - he didn't really have anything in mind when he told his lawyer to buy the property. But hosting three strangers for an indefinite period was not what he would ever have expected to happen.

"Why don't you stay for the weekend," Rami offered, "and we can keep talking. This is all still pretty new to me - to us, so I don't want to make any rash decisions. I hope you understand."

"Of course," Doc Hanover said with a smile. This wasn't a no! Which meant he was one step closer to yes, and rejoining the world of the living.

Or at least the world of the living dead.

"You can take my bed tonight," Willye said, standing and taking one of his bags, "and I'll take Wilson's. He can sleep on the couch. That boy can sleep anywhere." Taking the lead, she headed down the hallway towards her room, and he followed close behind, complimenting her on her dress. Which made her smile, but he could not see. It had been many, many years since a man complimented her attire.

"What do you think?" Brooke asked Rami.

"I think we should ask Willye," Rami said without hesitation.

Brooke looked down the hallway at them in her room. "I think I know what Willye's vote will be."

"How?" Rami asked.

Brooke rolled her eyes at him. "Are you serious?"

"What?" Then he got an inkling, "Were they flirting?"

"You're terrible. No wonder you can't get a boyfriend."

She winced. He laughed.

"Too soon?" she asked with a smile.

"A little too soon," he said, still laughing.

"Having fun?" Willye asked. Both jumped. Neither saw her return or heard her coming up behind them.

"What's your vote?" Rami asked her.

"My vote?"

"Well, you and Wilson live here. Brooke took part in the decision to let you guys stay. I figure you should be part of this decision."

Willye was flattered. She had so rarely been deferred to in life. It is, unsurprisingly, not a common occurrence in the life of a Black woman growing up in the 50s. "I think you - we should let him stay."

"Okay," Rami said with a smile.

"And then close that damn gate," she said over him. "We don't need to leave the red carpet rolled out for all to see."

Chapter Nine

This is a wild one. Like: wild. I didn't believe this one and wouldn't have if I hadn't found an interview with the professor herself.

Okay - so the video you are about to watch was taken by a student on campus not currently enrolled in Professor Chowdhury's Human Sexuality class at the time. Nor had they taken it before sneaking in, uninvited, to the After Class presentation.

The After Class presentations were optional. They did not contribute to your grade and were meant to give students access to resources and information on topics often found too taboo or difficult to find. They are almost always Rated R and sometimes Rated X. Still; the students are warned about the content beforehand and reminded at least three times before the presentation begins that it will be explicit. Those who will be uncomfortable or unable to handle the material with maturity should leave.

Word of this particular presentation spread far and wide, and one of the Christian clubs on campus decided they finally had the opportunity to get the class shut down. They had been trying to shut it down for years, but campus leadership never deemed the material too inappropriate.

This presentation would surely do the trick.

You can't hear what's being said but watch closely.

The petite woman with long blonde hair pulled up in an elastic band - the one sitting on the table naked, if you hadn't noticed - is Mallory.

You might think this is what the Christian club thought would get the class shut down. But you'd be wrong. It is, in fact, typical for Professor Chowdhury to hire consenting adults to perform live demonstrations, almost all requiring nudity. She believes it provides students with more realistic examples of healthy sexuality than what they learn watching porn. Her last book was about mental health issues Americans ignore because they are sexual in nature, thus making them nearly impossible to discuss. By normalizing sexuality and discussions of sex, as is her goal with these After Class demonstrations, people will be free to avoid the psychological harm done by sexual repression, abuse, or assault.

No, this class was unique because she planned to teach them how to use a vibrator on a woman.

Professor Chowdhury is the young woman wearing a kurti over jeans, holding a vibrator up for everyone to see. She always enjoyed taking pieces from her mother's traditional Indian clothing and adding them to her friends' American style. Prisha, of course, endured some ridicule from idiot boys. But she shut all that down one day when she proceeded to teach the boys some real insults, not the childish disappointments they constantly hurled her way. Some of the boys were so disturbed by her feedback that they told their parents, and Prisha was called down to the principal's office the next day to explain her use of such vile language.

Anyhow - back to the vibrator table where she's holding court. She has five different types of vibrators for the demonstration and walks the students through each vibrator's brand and unique qualities.

Mallory has performed in a few of these demonstrations, so the students are fairly desensitized to her. However, Professor Chowdhury is about to learn she's made a very problematic mistake. She is now calling for the other demonstrator, Bong Han. You see how she's looking left, off-stage? That's because she doesn't realize that the young man she hired as the second demonstrator is a student in her class, sitting in the audience.

Bong Han is the young man the other students are pushing to the front. He's first generation Korean-American. And he's also a virgin. The students don't know he's a virgin, but they all suspect it. He's become somewhat beloved, almost like the class mascot. It's because of his voice, you see. His voice is beautifully sonorous and deep. I mean deep. So it became a joke in class to ask Bong to repeat something someone said in a way that made it sound as sexual as possible. Bong wasn't an extrovert, but happy to have the attention. It didn't require anything of him; he just said things others said. Pretty easy. And it seemed some of the girls found him cute. He at least caught some of them looking at him, which was new. He started working out last semester to shed the boyish pudge he took to college with him, and it turned out he could grow a full beard.

Here's the moment where Prisha makes the decision that is going to send her career and his secondary education spiraling into the gutter. She pauses for a moment, having just figured out her error. She's debating whether to end the demonstration or proceed.

How she found herself in this position is actually quite simple: there are hundreds of students in her class, and Bong has never stayed for an After Class demonstration. If you've attended one of these (usually 100-level) courses in massive lecture halls packed to the brim with students - you can understand why she doesn't remember every single student in her class.

And Bong responded to the ad she posted, offering $100 to participate as a demonstrator. But, unfortunately, it never occurred to her to screen for current students.

Now the moment is over, the decision is made, their fates - at least on this day - are intertwined and carved in stone, and she hands him the first vibrator.

Bong takes the vibrator and… jams it into Mallory's pelvis. The class laughs, of course. Mallory takes his hand and guides the vibrator in for him; he shakes a bit and apologizes. As he speaks, her back arches. She takes the vibrator out of his hand and sets it aside. You can't hear what she is saying, but she's telling the class how important communication is when using a vibrator with a partner. She encourages Bong to keep talking. She invites him to reinsert the vibrator and does it this time with a much better aim. As she instructs him, his responses send little bolts of pleasure to her spine.

I'm not going to lie - even this probably would have been deemed acceptable by the university if Professor Chowdhury had run the idea past her department head. We all know what goes on on college campuses, and the more liberal the campus, the more it goes on. What you are about to hear is where the trouble begins:

Yes. That's a scream of pleasure from Mallory. It turns out Bong has a natural gift. And his nervous shaking is only making the sensation more intense.

Now those screams are because she just ejaculated on Bong. Most of the students had never seen anything like that before - those are the ones running out of the room. The ones who knew what was happening are the ones standing in silent awe.

That's where the video ends.

But that's not the last time you'll see Prisha and Bong.

Well, when Doc Hanover never left the ranch after his brief stop at Don's, the locals came to the correct assumption that he would be staying. They didn't need this assumption fact-checked. It was what they were going to assume, no matter what.

Even if the good doctor left town this very moment and shouted, "I'll never see you again!" as he drove out of town, there'd still be some who suspected he would return in the cover of night or fly in by helicopter. There is no limit to the imaginations of some people. Especially these people.

Needless to say, the locals started to get uneasy for the first time since Brooke and Rami moved in.

And Ralph was starting to enjoy the power that came with their suspicions and paranoia.

"So, they have seven rooms in that house," Ralph explained to the listeners at Don's. "That means there are two rooms left. Anyone think they aren't going to fill those rooms with folks like themselves? Outcasts?" No one said anything - but silence was agreement in Ralph's eyes, and he responded as such. "That doctor will not be the last."

"You don't think we could use a doctor closer to town?" Charlene asked from behind the bar. She just couldn't help herself.

Rayray shot her a look that she didn't quite understand but knew it meant she should stop talking pronto.

Ralph was a bit flustered. He wasn't used to being challenged and wasn't practiced in the art of using someone's argument against them.

But Rayray was.

"It won't just be a doctor. Sure, a doctor is nice. But it'll be others. Who don't care about our community, how we like to live? They'll build their mansions and condos and change everything."

"So, what do you propose we do about it?" Ray asked from the back of the room.

"I don't think we should do anything just yet,"

Ralph said. "But if any more people come to town, I think we should have a conversation with Rami about his intentions."

Everyone nodded in agreement.

Myles isn't your typical podcaster.

Or, at least, he doesn't think he is.

He is, of course, a typical podcaster.

He just happened to develop a following.

He built his following off of one viral episode when, by complete accident, he actually solved a murder.

His podcast isn't even a true crime podcast.

Shame Chasers is the name of his podcast, and each episode involves him interviewing individuals who our social media-fueled mob-mentality society canceled or publicly shamed. His dream interview is Monica Lewinsky.

In this particular episode, he interviewed an old millionaire who had been ostracized because everyone thought he killed his wife. He did kill his wife. But no one had ever been able to prove it.

Even Myles didn't realize he caught him until after his flight back to Seattle took off, and he listened to the recordings on the plane.

Near the end of the interview, Myles asked if he could use the bathroom.

"Up the stairs and to the right," the old man instructed.

Several seconds pass, and then: "This dumb cunt won't be able to figure out how I killed her either."

He had cataracts and couldn't see the phone screen sitting about two feet away from him. If he had been able to see it - he would have noticed that it was still recording.

But he couldn't. And didn't. And Myles got his big break.

And now he was on to his next story: Wilson's Catch.

He looked at the address in his notes and then up at the house that matched those coordinates. He tried not to make any noise while walking to the front door. He hoped to see if they were home before he knocked.

It didn't appear that anyone was home, so he knocked. When no one answered, he rang the doorbell and knocked again.

No one came to the door. He leaned over to see into their front window, and it looked dead inside.

"I think they moved away," he heard behind him, making him jump. "Sorry, didn't mean to scare you," the young woman said.

"That's okay. You said they moved?"

"No one knows for sure. But we haven't seen them around in a few weeks," she said. She stood there for a brief moment longer and then felt awkward. "Okay, bye," she said and walked away.

It wasn't uncommon for the people he wanted to interview to move. So he always did his research - and there had been no records of this property being put up for sale or sold.

He looked around for any indication of where they went.

That's when he saw the little UPS logo sticking out of the bush just below the front window. He reached down and pulled out a door tag for a missed UPS delivery. It was dated eighteen days ago with a box checked saying that delivery would be re-attempted the next day. He flipped it over. He smiled. Must not be too tech savvy, he thought to himself as he read the words PLEASE RE-ROUTE TO written in bold, perfect penmanship. Below those three words was an address.

"Why did she want this package sent to a town

in Montana?" he said to himself before pocketing the door tag and heading back to his rental car.

❖

Willye was sitting by herself on the porch, looking out at the barn. There wasn't any light pollution here in Montana, so she could see every star with crystal clarity. She couldn't remember the last time she'd been able to see the stars like that. A single bulb was on in the barn, hung by an extension cord from a rafter. She could barely distinguish the figures of Wilson and Brooke sweeping the floor.

"What's your favorite subject?" Brooke asked Wilson. He looked at her with suspicion. All kids grow up to be suspicious when adults ask them about school. Especially if they're asking about how they like school.

"I don't know," he said in a perfectly teenage way. He may only be twelve, but thirteen is around the corner, and he'd already started to grow a furrowed brow with his underarm hair.

Brooke rolled her eyes. She knew this game.

"Then... what's your favorite way to spend your time?"

"On my tablet," he shot back.

This is going to be fun, thought Brooke.

Then it occurred to her. He was still hiding under a layer of scar tissue. She remembered how hard the shaming had been for her as an adult... How can a kid handle that? she thought.

He can't.

So he hides.

She stopped sweeping.

"Do you know what happened to me?" she asked, suspecting he did.

He nodded. "Did you know about me?"

She thought for a moment before answering. She couldn't be sure whether the truth would make him feel better or worse.

She decided to go with the truth: "No, not really."

He raised his eyebrows in surprise at this. It had been over a year since he met someone who didn't know about his catch. But he didn't say anything in response. She didn't know what he was thinking, so she went back to sweeping.

"Nothing like it, is there?" Doc Hanover asked from the front door, looking up at the sky. Willye turned and smiled at him.

"I know exactly what you mean," she said and

patted next to her on the bench. It took him a couple attempts to sit, but he managed. His knees aren't as good as they used to be. And moving to a more rugged terrain might not be the best for them. But it sure is better than the loneliness and shame.

"So you and your wife were married for..." Willye started for him.

"Forty-two years," he replied with pride.

Willye let out a whistle that said Hot damn! since she wouldn't ever say such a thing out loud. "You two must have been very happy together."

"We were." Then he went quiet. At her age, Willye knows when there are no words to be said, and silence speaks the truth loudest. So she patted his hand and set her gaze back on the barn.

"I didn't even see it until the last second," Wilson said out of the blue. Brooke was halted by this sudden moment of personal sharing but knew that if she didn't respond quickly enough and in the exact right way, then the moment would be gone, and he'd close up for who knows how many months before trying to connect again. By that point, he might not even be living with them.

"I didn't even remember sending that tweet,"

Brooke offered. "It was such a tiny moment and meant nothing to me. When I heard the news, I didn't know what they were talking about because it never occurred to me that one of my tweets might be at the heart of the matter."

"Yeah. It happened so quickly. One second I'm sitting with my grandma; the next, a ball is heading my way, just feet away, and I don't even remember deciding to catch it. I just shoved my glove out, and it went in." He stood there silently for a few seconds. "I was just so happy to catch a fly ball."

She walked over and put her arm around him.

"Why are people so mean?" he asked.

"It means they are unhappy in their lives and only feel better when others feel worse," she said without thinking. She surprised herself. She came up with that so quickly and easily. Because you're a writer, she told herself.

Used to be a writer, she corrected.

"Were you married?" Doc Hanover asked Willye.

"Noooo. Not that I didn't want to. But God had different plans for me," she said without emotion.

"What were those plans?" he asked.

She pointed to the barn, at the silhouette of Brooke hugging Wilson.

"His mama wasn't supposed to happen the way she did," Willye said. And that was all.

The Doc could infer what he wanted from that, she thought. The truth was too awful, and she never wanted Wilson to learn about his mother's past. Having lived his mother's - albeit brief - adulthood, he already went through too many trials and tribulations. He'd come out the other side okay and proven that he was more than his and his mother's genetics.

"You took him when his mother passed?"

"Mm mm. His mother is still alive, but... not with us anymore. If you know what I mean."

He nodded. The opioid crisis had ravaged New England, and he saw too many of his patients slide into that black hole. He didn't know if drugs had taken over Wilson's mother's life - but he was familiar with the sentiment of someone being "alive" but "no longer with us" at the same time. Their body still moved around the planet, but inside, it was no longer the person they knew.

"His father?" Doc inquired.

"He's back in Nigeria," she said quickly before

pivoting with, "I've never lived anywhere where you could see stars like these."

Doc knew what that meant. There was a story there, but not one she wished to tell tonight. Which was perfectly fine with the Doc.

Unseen by the four, Rami stood at one of the windows and watched Doc and Willye conversing and Brooke hugging Wilson.

This is right, he thought to himself.

After all of their lives had been upended and obliterated, they could finally find an empathetic ear rather than a pitying one. They could connect with human beings again, but those who actually understood them.

This is nice, he thought. Peace. Finally.

And this was indeed the most peaceful night any of them had had in almost a year and more for some of them.

"Dinner's ready!" Rami shouted, knocking the screen door off its hinges in the process.

"Looks like we have a new project, Wilson!" Brooke said with her arm around his shoulder as they walked to the house.

Looking at Rami smiling, I want to warn him that this is their last peaceful night.

You see, they only get one.

Because tomorrow, a knock on the door will change everything.

Dinner began as it always begins, with Willye saying grace silently while everyone sort of waits for her. Willye doesn't expect anyone to say grace with her, nor does she expect them to wait for her. And she has told them this several times.

Until one night, Brooke asked Willye, "Would your family wait for you to say grace before eating?"

Willye thought for a moment before nodding, "Yes, I suppose they would."

"Then that's why we're waiting," Brooke said, not noticing the smile creeping onto Wilson's face.

Tonight was Rami's night to cook, which meant no green beans or collard greens, no sweet potatoes or corn on the cob, no slow-cooked Boston butt or grilled salmon.

No. It meant homemade pizza with a salad from a bag.

"Rami!" Brooke scolds him.

"What?!" Rami asks in faux surprise, though the faux embarrassment is only half-faux.

"Son, you should have spent less time on the computer and more time in the kitchen," Doc Hanover said with a wink to Willye, which made her laugh so hard she spit out her drink.

"What?" Doc laughed.

"You're bad," Willye says with an eye-roll. "Speaking of bad…"

Wilson slouches in his chair a tad. He's lucky he hasn't hit that growth spurt yet, or no amount of slouching would hide him.

"I don't see why I need Algebra…" Wilson pouted under his breath. Willye wanted to respond but couldn't come up with anything fast enough. So Brooke jumped in.

"Rami? Did you take algebra?" Brooke asked, giving him a look that let him know the answer was yes, no matter the truth.

"I did…" Rami responded, not sure where Brooke was taking him.

"Well, Wilson here could use some encouragement," she said, her eyes looking up from her plate, locked on Wilson.

"Let's take a crack at it after dinner, Wilson," Rami suggested, to which Wilson responded with a classic Willye-eye-roll that she would have been proud of had it not been in defiance to her.

"Young man…" Willye started before Wilson shot back, "Why? So I can go to college? Get a job? Who's going to say yes to me?"

The group sat in silence for a few seconds taking in the weight of this young man's emotional burden. Then Doc spoke up.

"Maybe no one, that's true," he started. Wilson was about to interject, so doc Hanover pushed through, "but you don't know that. None of us know what comes next. But I can't imagine this is… forever, and nor should you."

Wilson took this in, not looking at Doc, and began eating again. The group followed, and the moment had almost passed when Wilson said under his breath, "I don't know, I wish this place was forever."

Looking at Rami smiling at Wilson's comment, I want to warn him that this is their last peaceful night. To enjoy this while he can. But I can't.

"Well, I've put together a list of all the repairs we still need to make," Brooke said, changing the subject.

"Doc'll get right on those," Willye said, nudging the good doctor in the ribs.

"I can get some guys out here…" Rami starts to respond before Brooke cuts him off.

"Why don't we do it ourselves?" The group looks at her in silence. "I mean, not all of it. I don't mean we dig up and replace the septic system. But like fixing doors, simple electrical wiring, painting. I know I'd like to change the color of my bedroom…" she said, trying to cue others with the same desire. No one bit, but everyone nodded at the sentiment.

"I just don't want to burden you all… you didn't pick this place; I did… faults and all…" Rami stammered.

"But this is our home, Rami," Brooke explained.

"And we want to help," Doc chimed in.

"Thank you," Rami said simply and earnestly. "I don't think I've ever had a home," he realized aloud.

Willye placed her hand on Rami's arm and smiled. "It's been a very long time since we had one." Brooke put her arm around Wilson.

I'm glad they got this night together. They all deserved to feel what it is to have a home and belong to a family again. If only they knew to savor it.

You see, things won't go as they expect, just as Doc Hanover told Wilson.

Because tomorrow, a knock on the door will change everything.

Chapter Ten

Here it comes. I told you it would happen. And the moment is here.

The footsteps walking up the front porch steps were too quiet to hear inside the house.

But what came next was not:

A knock at the front door.

It was early, and no work had been scheduled today, so nobody was expected at the house. And it was a bit out of the way for anyone going door-to-door evangelizing or selling knives for week-end beer money.

Wilson heard the knock from the barn, Brooke from her bedroom upstairs, Rami from the kitchen, Willye from the living room, and Doc Hanover returning from his morning walk.

"Can I help you?" Doc Hanover asked from

behind Myles. Startled, Myles turned around so fast he dropped his phone.

Fumbling around in the early morning light, Myles found his phone and started recording with one swipe and tap.

"I'm Myles Pendergast," he said and then paused. He was waiting for recognition. He didn't get any from the good doctor. Doc Hanover is not much of a podcast listener. I'm not sure he even knows what a podcast is.

"What can I do for you, Myles?" Doc Hanover said, making sure Myles knew he heard his name but not offering his own. In a few seconds, though, he will find out he didn't need to tell him his name.

"Are you Doctor Hanover?" Myles asked, even though he knew the answer. He didn't see any value in pretending he wasn't there to get their story, so he decided to jump in head-first.

"Mm hm?" Doc Hanover replied. Where is this going, he thought.

As Myles explained his presence, Wilson came out of the barn to investigate the knocking and conversation coming from the porch.

"I host a podcast that tells the true stories of

fine folks who have been shamed into…" he looked around them, "… hiding," he concluded.

He always assures them his goal is to tell their true story because everyone he wants to interview feels that their story has been misconstrued and often leaps at the opportunity to "set the record straight." His goal isn't to tell their true story, though. If that's what happens, it's icing on the cake. But his real goal is always to get as many listens and shares as possible. And each episode is crafted with great precision as the means to that end.

"How's everything going, Doc?" Rami asked from the front door, wearing a bathrobe and slippers. He hadn't heard everything Myles said, but he had a pretty good idea of what he wanted. He came here looking for a story.

Myles turned around and offered his hand, "Myles Pendergast," he said and then paused.

Still no recognition, but Rami shook it. "Rami. What can we do for you?"

"He's casting something," Doc Hanover explained with complete inaccuracy.

"I host a popular podcast…" Myles began.

"Wilson!" Willye shouted from inside.

"He's out here, Willye!" Rami shouted to her. "I'm sorry," he said, turning to Myles, "you were saying?"

Myles didn't respond. He had just realized that the young man over by the barn was the Wilson he wanted to interview.

Before he could start speaking, Willye came out of the house with a paper bag in one hand and a bowl of green beans in the other. "Help me trim these green beans!" she shouted to Wilson, not even noticing Myles' presence. She parked herself on the bench, set the bowl on the seat beside her so it would be between her and Wilson, and placed the paper bag in front of her. Without another word, she began snapping off the ends of the beans and tossing them into the paper bag. Everyone watched. Myles tried to understand what on earth was happening.

"Do you all..." Myles began, his brain whirring and clicking away, "... live here? Together?"

Rami put his hand on Myles' shoulder and guided him down the front stairs. "We're not interested in talking..." he began.

"But what... why? How did you meet?" Myles

kept rambling even as Rami walked him almost entirely to his car.

"Look," Rami said, releasing his shoulder and looking him square in the eyes, "we are just looking for some peace and quiet. I'm sure you can appreciate that."

Rami looked back to the group. Wilson had joined Willye on the bench and was snapping bean ends like a pro, with Doc Hanover now standing on the porch next to Willye, whispering an overview of how Myles wanted to cast something. It only confused the poor woman. Hopefully, someone will explain podcasts to him someday. Maybe Wilson.

"Sure, sure. I understand," Myles said, not paying complete attention to the words coming out of Rami's mouth as he was still processing what he had just stumbled upon.

"Thank you," Rami said and started heading back to the porch.

"What's going on out here?" Brooke asked, stepping out onto the porch.

The sight of Brooke - the person responsible for Rami's shaming and who was then shamed when Rami came out - nearly broke Myles' brain.

An idea struck. He pulled out his phone and opened the camera app. "If you ever change your mind," he called out to them. This had the desired effect: Rami turned around.

And in a half-second, Myles took a photo of the five. This is it, he thought with a smile.

"Hey!" Rami started to protest. But Myles was already in his car and pulling away, spraying a dirt cloud behind him in haste.

While Charlene appreciated the business, the unfamiliar faces that appeared at the diner this morning baffled her.

Charlene, you see, is not a podcast listener. I don't know how many people are. I'm not. I tried many times. I don't know. It just doesn't stick. Surely some people must listen to them, or why would anyone make them? Unless the entire podcast listening audience is made up entirely of podcasters? Who knows. Probably someone.

What I'm getting at is that Charlene had not heard Myles' podcast. She was unaware that it had been popular. It didn't necessarily "go viral" - it didn't surpass his most listened-to episode. But it received a healthy number of listens and caught the attention of some reporters.

Those reporters, so it would seem, brought their unfamiliar faces to town and made their way to the diner after listening to the episode. Or maybe they were assigned the story. It doesn't matter.

What matters is that Charlene is quite adept at eavesdropping and making conversation and knows exactly what is going on by the end of her shift.

"What brings you to town?" she asked one of the women sitting by herself.

"Oh, work. I'm a writer." That was all she said. And to make sure that Charlene knew she didn't want to talk further, she smiled while she put in her earbuds and shifted her focus to her phone screen.

Now you can see why it took Charlene almost her entire shift before she understood the whole story.

Her big breakthrough came when a new, unfamiliar face walked in and recognized one of the other unfamiliar faces. "Ryan! Good to see you," he said, walking over to the table where, ostensibly,

Ryan sat. Fortunately for him, it was Ryan. And fortunately for Charlene, she now knew one of their names!

"You been up to the house yet?" the unfamiliar face asked Ryan as he took off his coat.

"No," Ryan said, the disappointment thick in his voice. "They have the gate closed."

"And there's no way around it?" asked the unfamiliar face.

"I started walking the fence, but it just takes you farther away from the house. I gave up after about 10 minutes and headed back to the car."

"They probably shut it after what's-his-name showed up."

What's-his-name is Myles Pendergast.

"Don't blame them. Who wants a bunch of reporters showing up on their front porch?"

"Our editors," Ryan replied. They both found the joke hysterically funny. I don't get it, but I'm not a reporter.

Reporters, Charlene clocked.

"Have you been able to get in touch with any of the people he interviewed?" asked the unfamiliar face.

"Not yet." He pulled out a notebook and

removed the elastic band keeping it shut. "I'm waiting until that bar... what's the one? Where what's-his-name interviewed..."

"Don's," Ryan answered.

"Yeah, I'm waiting until Don's opens." You see, the unfamiliar face did not know the secret buzz and was unaware of how to get Don to open Don's any hour of the day. "Seems like a good chance they'll be there after work."

Myles' podcast had not featured their "true story" after all. Not that anyone was surprised. Not that any of them listened to it. Because they didn't. Even when it came out, a week after he visited the property, Doc Hanover still did not understand that Myles had not been casting anything.

He only captured a few minutes of recording time with the group, and much of it was muffled. So he decided to interview the locals.

And the locals were more than happy to be interviewed on their favorite topic to gripe about.

The story that came together was about how opaque the farmhouse residents were about their intentions. They seemed nice enough, but not one of them could tell you how long they would be there or what they planned to do once they had the property fixed up.

He featured Ralph quite a bit, as well as Rayray. The two did not miss a single opportunity to speak into the microphone.

It's good that Rami did not listen to the podcast, or he would have been infuriated. He will be infuriated when he listens to it a few months from now. But by that point, he and the other four would be living quite differently from how they did now. So he takes a hit from the bong Doc Hanover bought them and lets it roll off him.

Oh yeah. Doc Hanover is a heavy consumer of cannabis and not only introduces Rami to it but makes him his cannabis connoisseur protege. But that's later.

Ryan pulled his wallet out of his pocket and removed a $20. Dropping it on the table, he stood up and said, "Alright, I'm going to head over to that gas station. I'm meeting um…" He tried to recall Gerry's name. "Gary! That's it." It isn't. "When I swung by earlier, the cashier said he would be in about half an hour ago."

"Good seeing you, Ryan," the unfamiliar face

said before returning his attention to his notebook.

"Have a safe flight if I don't see you again, Chuck," Ryan said to the unfamiliar face whose name Charlene now knew to be Chuck.

Charlene decided to use this moment to make small talk with Chuck.

"You here for the ranch?" she asked Chuck.

"Do you know any of them?" Chuck asked with hopeful excitement.

"Oh, no. I don't know any of them personally," she said. And then it occurred to her: "I've never met any of them, now that I think of it."

"They don't come into the diner?"

"They don't really spend much time in town," she corrected him. Chuck wrote this down in his notebook. "What got you interested in them?"

"My editor heard the podcast and sent me out here," he explained.

"That makes sense," she said. Though it didn't. She didn't know what podcast he was talking about. But she thought it would be better to play like she did so that, hopefully, he'd keep talking.

"Anyhow, that brings me out here," Chuck

said. And then, flirting, he asked, "What brings you here?"

Charlene has no patience for flirting. So she smiled, said, "Work, silly!" and walked away.

Well, she wouldn't get any more out of him. Once a man turns his attention to trying to seduce someone, there isn't much else his brain will do.

In total, seven unfamiliar faces, two of whom were Ryan and Chuck, made their way to the diner throughout Charlene's shift.

Not a single one would get an interview with any of the five at the farmhouse. But that didn't bother them so much as, once again, the locals were more than happy to speak endlessly on the topic.

❖

Gerry had come to enjoy the added business the ranch residents brought in with their deliveries and such. But today, he was having an even better day than usual.

Which perplexed him.

And when Gerry was perplexed, it unnerved him.

Gerry isn't used to being unnerved.

He has served in the Gulf War, been through

recessions, been laid off more times than he can remember, and experienced a brutal divorce from the woman he met in the Gulf War who left him when he was laid off during the 2008 recession.

If that doesn't help you build up grit and resilience, well... then I think you're fucked.

Gerry would agree with me.

But Gerry is resilient, and he isn't fucked - though life had certainly given its best shot at fucking him - and the unnerved feeling he was feeling at that very moment did not sit well with him.

While standing behind the counter, absent-mindedly staring at a carton of cigarettes in his hand, Ron came in and thought, What's up with Gerry?

"What's up with you, Gerry?" he asked. Gerry didn't respond. "Gerry?" Gerry snapped out of whatever was mesmerizing him. It didn't occur to Ron that Gerry may be in deep thought. Ron didn't have deep thoughts that often. So it didn't occur to him that others might be in the middle of one.

"Oh, just deep in thought, I guess," Gerry replied. Ron, as you know, didn't know what that meant. So he asked.

"What's that mean?"

Gerry looked at the carton of cigarettes in his hand with confusion before setting them down in a random place since he didn't know where he'd gotten them from.

"I guess..." Gerry started. "I don't know. Just some folks that have come through today. Not the usual delivery trucks."

"More reporters?" Ron guessed.

"No. They didn't seem like reporters. Like they were here for work."

Something gnawed at the back of his brain, and he couldn't quite identify it.

"Think they're visiting someone here?" Gerry offered.

And that did, in fact, dislodge the synapse chewing away in the background of Gerry's mind.

Suitcases. They had suitcases with them. And if they weren't visiting someone, then there could only be one other destination they could have in mind.

As he arrived at this conclusion - a Jeep rolled up to the Number 4 pump. He and Ron couldn't make out the faces of the people through the old, waxy windows of the gas station. But when the strangers opened the back of the Jeep, he could see it was crammed with suitcases and bags.

"I think you need to get down to Don's, Ron," Gerry said.

Ron was confused. "Why's that?"

"I think these folks are planning to move into that farmhouse," Gerry said. And as he spoke those words, he could feel the truth in them. He knew he was correct. "That's the third car to come through here, packed to the brim like that. I don't know any other reason a stranger would come to town carting that much stuff."

I didn't tell you about this knock. I wanted to keep it a surprise for you.

But if Myles' knock set these events into motion, the knock about to meet their front door is gas being poured on the fire.

A great conflagration is upon us!

And nobody touched by it will ever be the same.

And that's when it happened:

A knock at the front door.

Rami and Brooke were unpacking some boxes they "hadn't had time to unpack" until now. If you've moved in your adult life, you know exactly what I'm talking about. We all still have that one box somewhere in an attic or basement or closet or storage space that we know we should have unpacked by now but "just haven't gotten to it."

So, like many of us, Rami and Brooke finally got around to putting the contents of these last boxes away.

As the knock reverberated through the still-mostly-unfurnished farmhouse, Rami opened a most fortuitous box indeed: Brooke's dishes.

They hadn't needed her dishes because they had unpacked Rami's, and he owned exactly two sets of dishes.

Rami's prior life required no more than two of everything. He did own a lot of silverware, but that's only because you can't buy silverware in pairs easily.

But five of them occupied the farmhouse now. And eating became a bit of a juggling act as they improvised with bowls for plates and mugs for cups.

About 37 minutes before the knock, Willye and Doc Hanover took off on one of their evening walks. Roughly 2 minutes before that, Willye rolled her eyes when Wilson informed her he preferred to stay home and play on his tablet. It was his reference to the farmhouse as home that stopped her from insisting he get out of the house and play like other kids his age. She clearly did not spend time around many other kids Wilson's age. So she let him stay.

And only Rami and Brooke heard the knock.

When they heard the knock, Brooke and Rami looked at each other. They said nothing, but their looks communicated that it excited neither of them to find out who was at the door and that they should go together. So they did.

Before opening the door, Brooke looked through the peephole to see if they recognized the person. She didn't and gestured to Rami to look. He, too, did not recognize the couple standing on the porch. They looked at each other and shrugged. The shrug said, "Fuck it."

Also, the floors of that house creaked, so the two on the porch certainly heard them walk up to the door. It would be weird not to open it.

Rami opened the door. "Hi," he said, and that was it. The two started to smile. "Yes?" he prodded them.

Neither the woman nor the young man said

anything at first. It seemed that they weren't sure who struck Prisha speechless. But the speechlessness wore off soon, and she found herself able to use her voice.

"I'm Prisha Chowdhury; this is Bong Han. It's so nice to meet you two," she said, and a considerable weight seemed to lift off her shoulders.

"Rami," he offered with his hand. He looked at their car, trying to figure out how they made it up to the house. He closed the gate earlier.

"Brooke," she said with an eye-roll that implied, of course they know who I am. Which they did. So eye-rolled correctly.

"I used to read your finance articles," Prisha said. "It's too bad..." she started to say. What she stopped herself from saying was that it was too bad that nobody published Brooke's writing anymore. But that seemed both evident and a sore subject - and she pivoted to a new sentence: "It's too bad that I'm getting to meet you under these circumstances."

Ah, Rami thought.

Prisha saw that Rami understood and waited for him to say something. She hoped he'd say something.

He didn't.

She didn't know exactly how to proceed from here - so she pulled out her phone and pulled up the infamous video. She handed it to Rami. He hesitated at first. He couldn't decide if he wanted to watch whatever she was handing him to watch.

Brooke, on the other hand, never missed out on an opportunity for something juicy - so she reached over and tapped the play icon hovering over the preview image.

The preview image showed Bong holding a vibrator while Prisha sits on the table with a blurry cloud over her crotch.

Rami didn't focus on the video, though. He stared at the millions of views the video had accumulated. He found it remarkable that in this over-connected age, it was still possible for an event to be recorded and viewed millions of times and yet still be unknown by much of the population. He had not seen this video before nor heard of their story.

As Brooke watched, a memory hit her hard, and she suddenly remembered hearing about this story.

"You're the student?!" she asked Bong.

He demurred.

Prisha blushed.

She caught herself blushing and jumped back into what they wanted to discuss:

"The university dismissed me, and no other schools will even give me an interview," Prisha told them.

"What about you?" Rami asked Bong.

"They expelled you, right?" Brooke answered for him.

"Yeah," Bong said before hanging his head in shame.

Bong tried not to dwell on this fact too much. He was on track for an incredible career in structural engineering. He dreamed of helping design structures that seemed to defy physics yet were the product of physics. A building that appeared to stand upside down on the peak of its roof. A high rise that seemed to lean but was, in fact, a perfect 90 degrees from the ground.

I'm not sure if he will ever get to do any of these things. He doesn't while he's here at the ranch.

Though, he does get to put his skills and education to use in unexpected ways.

Well, I guess the cat's out of the bag. Now

you know that Rami and Brooke are going to let them stay.

So I guess we can skip past this awkward porch talk and jump right to the deal-making.

Rami invited them to sit on the bench, and he and Brooke sat across from them in two somewhat broken plastic chairs.

"Can I ask…" Rami started, "How did you get up here?"

Prisha seemed baffled by this question. "The gate was open."

Well, now we know where Willye and Doc went on their walk, he thought. I need to remind them to always close and lock the gate if they leave that way.

"Right," Rami said, pretending this had been his choice.

"So… do you need…" she began. She didn't know how to ask how many rooms they needed politely. "Do you two need… uh," she came up with.

"No!" Prisha and Bong said in unison as they figured out the real question. They looked at each other and laughed.

"I'm a lesbian," Prisha shared. "While it may have appeared on the video…" She ended the sentence there. "Anyhow, no, we're not together." And then she felt the right moment open before her: "But we are hoping the last two rooms are still available."

Last two rooms? thought Rami. Clearly, they did their research. Prisha noticed this change in him.

Prisha, you see, is one of the most observant people I've ever met. She can tell you things you never knew or would have guessed about yourself. Her original calling - or at least that's how she thought of it - was psychology. She played the role of amateur therapist for her friends and family growing up. So, it seemed logical that she should become a therapist or go into another field in psychology. Psychiatry didn't interest her, though her parents hoped she might change her mind in school.

Both of her parents were psychiatrists.

"How did you know we have two rooms unoccupied?" Rami asked. He didn't want to call them available as that implied someone would definitely stay in them.

"I read in some articles that there are five of you up here, so I looked up the property and house in public records," she answered, "hoping that there might be room for us here too."

"Well, that isn't just my decision. Brooke and I need to talk about this with the others."

"Of course!" Prisha assured him.

That's when the backdoor that led into the kitchen opened, and Doc Hanover called, "Rami! Rami!"

Brooke and Rami reacted in milliseconds and dashed into the kitchen, leaving their potential new housemates on the porch.

Doc Hanover looked like he had been running, or at least speed walking - his cheeks flushed, and his hair matted with sweat. "Cars are pulling up at the gate!" he shouted and pointed.

They went out the backdoor, and Willye stood about 50 feet away, looking down the driveway. When they reached her - she pointed at the gate in the distance.

Rami could see one car parked; people pulling things out of it. And it looked like another car planned to park by the gate.

"What do we do?" Brooke asked Rami.

Rami stood there thinking.

"We go down and meet them," he said and started down the driveway.

On occasion, the universe is wont to rhyme, and as the meeting of Prisha and Bong took place on the farmhouse porch, Ralph headlined a hullabaloo down at Don's, working the locals up into a tizzy.

About 15 minutes back, Ron ran into the bar and told them that three cars of strangers hauling suitcases had come through the gas station just now, and Gerry suspected they were heading to the ranch.

A silence, unusual to this place, followed. Unusual enough, in fact, that Don came rushing in from the back room to see what happened. "Is everything alright?!" he asked in a panic.

"Nope," Ralph said.

And with that one word, he became the group's unofficial leader.

Ralph's nonchalance while confirming that something was wrong confused Don.

Don began to ask, "What's wrong?" but Ralph saw this question coming and jumped to the answer before the question could be asked:

"I'll tell you what's wrong. People from cities around this country are moving here. And not normal people. Good people. People ostracized by their community, family, and friends." Ralph learned the word ostracized from Rayray. Hearing it in use, Rayray smiled to himself.

"How do you know that?" Don asked.

"Gerry's seen three cars come through the gas station," Ron explained. This helped nothing. Don's confusion only increased. So Ralph stepped in.

"All three were packed with suitcases. And not a one of them was recognizable," Ralph clarified. "If that doesn't look like they're planning on staying, I don't know what would."

The men all nodded.

"They gotta be out of rooms," Don said, offering a reason to stay calm.

"They've got an entire ranch," Ray spoke up.

"So they're going to put people up in, what, the barns?" Don pointed out. "Where would they live? You can't survive a winter in Montana camping outdoors."

"He's a millionaire!" Ralph reminded everyone.

"Who?" Bart asked.

Everyone stared at Bart. Rayray shook his head with the shame only a sibling can feel when their little brother says something so idiotic.

"Rami, Bart," Rayray said, losing his patience. "Rami!"

"Wait a minute. He's a millionaire?!" Bart replied and made Rayray want to put his head in a bag.

"I think we're getting off-topic here," Rayray said with a look to Ralph that urged him to get everyone back on track.

"My point," Ralph said, raising his voice to focus everyone's attention again, "is that it doesn't matter what is on that property currently. He can build a hundred mansions if he wants to!"

"But why would he do that?" Don asked.

"Because he can," Ralph replied.

"But there's no need..." Don started to say before Rayray cut him off.

"Only a few months ago, none of them lived there, right?" Rayray asked the room. Everyone nodded. "Then there were two of them. Fine, not a big deal. Another, what, month or so later, three more join them. When was the last time five unrelated people moved here?" No one knew the answer.

"I can't remember," Don admitted, "And I'm the oldest one here."

"See?" Ralph said to the group. "So we already have a… a… what's the word, Rayray?"

"Anomaly," Rayray assisted.

"Right! We already have an anomaly…"

"Shut your mouth!" Rayray whispered to Bart when he saw the young man about to say something embarrassing.

"… and we know of at least three more cars of people headed up there. That means at least three more people. That brings it to eight. It took two months to go from two people to five, and only two weeks to go from five to eight." Ray waited for everyone to see the pattern. "I don't think we should get comfy thinking that we won't see five or ten more people showing up tomorrow!"

"How likely is that? Really?" Don asked.

"Why do you care so much, Don? None of them spend a cent in this bar," Rayray challenged.

Now, Don did not want to find himself on the opposite side of this argument from everyone else. But he also spent his career behind this bar acting as most of these guys' unofficial therapist. So he knew them well enough to know they could get wound up about almost anything if given enough time.

He also knew that Ralph had grown more paranoid, suspicious, and ornery with every year since JuliEtta's death. Her death changed Ralph. Sure, all deaths change the people close to them - but JuliEtta's death was not just something to mourn. It resulted from city doctors not giving a flying fuck about folks like them. Or, at least, that's what Ralph believed.

In truth, there was no saving JuliEtta. And while, yes, many of the doctors they visited did not demonstrate the best bedside manner and often talked over his head, every one of them accurately diagnosed her and offered the same plan forward. But Ralph got stuck when they started talking over his head. It is his greatest pet peeve. He hates when people speak to him in a way that makes them look more intelligent than he is. Even if they were more educated than he on the subject - such as this situation - it didn't matter to Ralph. The fact that they didn't try to help him understand infuriated him to this day. It meant he didn't matter to them.

He wasn't worth communicating with. He was just some dumb country lump-on-a-log who couldn't understand their highfalutin genius, so they might as well speak fast and get it over with.

I genuinely believe that if even one of the oncologists they met with took the time to help him understand what was happening to JuliEtta and how even modern medicine is not robust enough to save most people with ovarian cancer, the events I'm laying out before you would never happen.

But the loss of JuliEtta also took away Ralph's stabilizer. She alone could pull him back from the brink when he got worked up. She could talk logic into him. She could get him to calm down with just a look.

So it was inevitable that Ralph would not fare well after she passed. But he didn't need to go down this path.

Here's the thing: I know for a fact that if Ralph did not go down the path he is barreling along, he would never find someone who could bring that stability into his life. In a completely unexpected way.

As impossible as it may seem right now from

everything shared with you, these events set Ralph on a path that will improve his life in ways he never imagined. I can't tell him that, though it would be nice to assure him that his world is not ending, even if the world as he knows it is coming to a close before the end of this year.

Back to the question Rayray posed to Don: why does he care so much when none of the newcomers patronize his bar?

"Look, I just don't want unnecessary trouble. That's all," Don said, trying to get his back out of a corner. It wasn't a good response to Rayray's question. It was more of deflection. But as Don learned over the years, deflection is an excellent strategy to employ on these guys. Especially when they're wound up. Don't give them anything to hang onto; they'll move on back to whatever business they were up to and forget about the awkward moment altogether. Which is precisely what happened.

"I think that's what we're all saying," Ray chimed in.

Don went to respond but thought better of it.

Ralph felt a sense of pride when Ray spoke up and supported him. His whole life, he looked up to Ray as an older brother. He didn't have any siblings himself, and the Mulfords acted more like family to him than his own parents. His dad excelled at being a violent asshole, and Ralph had no one else to share the beatings with - so he spent as little time at home as possible and as much time at the Mulfords as they would allow. Which was most of the time.

"So we're all in agreement?" Ralph asked the group. Everyone, including Don, nodded. Though Don's nod was a little more subdued. Rayray nodded so emphatically with agreement you could probably feel it in Texas.

"What do you think we should do about it?" Ray asked Ralph.

"I think we should go talk to them and find out their intentions," Ralph said after some thought.

"You think they'll tell the truth?" Dickie asked. The way he asked it implied that he did not think they would be. "Why wouldn't they lie to us?"

This was just the sort of poison that no one needed injected into Ralph's brain. But injected it had been and infected his brain now was.

"You gotta good point there, Dickie," Ralph said and took a seat at the bar, turning his stool around to face the group. Rayray walked over and stood next to him. He wanted to be seen as Ralph's second in command, and he thought standing by his side would give that impression. Sort of like a knight standing beside the monarch they are protecting.

The room again fell unusually silent. All eyes focused on Ralph.

Ralph had never experienced this much power. It was intoxicating. It is unfortunate, then, that Ralph's intoxication with power will be his undoing, as it is for many white men who find themselves in an intoxicating position of power.

Ralph pondered in the silence but enjoyed the attention he held and entertained the idea of holding his silence even after he completed his ponder.

Rayray became a little nervous that Ralph was taking too long and would soon lose the group's attention. "Whatcha thinking, Ralph?" he asked.

"I think we need to make an impression," Ralph said.

"Intimidation?" Ray inquired.

"Impression," Bart corrected Ray with wild inaccuracy.

Ray yanked Bart's hat off his head in one seamless movement and smacked him with it.

"I mean: should we try intimidating them?" he said to get Bart on the same page as the rest.

"There's only five of them," Dickie pointed out. The others considered this.

"You're not thinking of doing anything…" Don started to say.

"Don, all ideas are on the table, and you're more than welcome to start contributing rather than asking asshat questions from behind your bar!" Rayray said without looking Don's way.

"Ray, Rayray, Dickie - you three follow me in your trucks," Ralph instructed. "Bart and Ron…"

"I'm technically still on the clock…" Ron started to say before Ralph continued.

"Bart and Ron, you can ride with those three," Ralph concluded.

"Gerry's probably fine," Ron justified to himself.

Ralph took a look around the room. "Ready?"

Everyone nodded. Except for Bart. Bart shouted, "Ready!"

As the group streamed out of the bar and to their trucks, Don felt a sinking feeling in his stomach. Something told him that none of them would be the same after going down this path. That they were about to start something that tore the town apart, or worse. It could lead to violence.

Don grabbed a pint glass and did something with it he seldom does: he filled it up and took a drink.

As Brooke and Rami walked down the driveway to the gate, Rami started to slow his pace.

"Everything okay?" Brooke asked him. She was so attuned to his changes that it shocked him sometimes.

"I don't know?" he said without looking at her.

"We don't have to go talk to them," she said, offering him an out.

"Yes, we do," he said.

"Why?"

"Because they're like us. And how would you feel if we were on the other side of that gate and nobody came to let us in?"

Brooke nodded. What would she have done if Rami hadn't offered her a room at the farmhouse? Moved back in with her parents. That's what.

And then she started to think about Willye and Wilson. How she made Wilson laugh while they cleaned out the barn. How Willye had started to slough off her protective shell and open up. Even more so since Doc Hanover arrived.

It occurred to her that all of them had been renewed by their time at the farmhouse, even as brief a time as it had been.

Because we feel seen again, she thought.

She never understood before what people meant when they said they felt seen. She found the phrase so strange. Of course you can be seen. How could you not be? she often thought.

Brooke knew very well that her shaming was the easiest of the five of them. She started living in Montana with Rami about a month after hers. The others lived with theirs for much longer. She couldn't even begin to imagine what it had been like for Willye and Wilson.

But even living in public under the shame for only a few weeks, Brooke could appreciate what it meant to be seen.

The world did not actually know Brooke. They knew the version of her that social media re-defined into an over-simplistic meme. A sound bite. That is who she is to most human beings. That is what they see. They don't see her.

Rami did, though. As did Willye, Wilson, and Doc.

Brooke took Rami's hand. She had a new appreciation for what this house, this ranch, meant. What it represented. What it offered people like them. Rami looked down at their hands and back at Brooke.

"Don't worry, I know I'm not your type," she said with a wink. Rami laughed.

About three hundred feet from the gate, the people on the other side started waving to them. Rami and Brooke gave a warm wave back to assure them they came as friends, not to kick them off the property.

"What do I say to them?" Rami asked Brooke in a sudden panic.

"Hi, I'm Rami. You are?" Brooke suggested with an eye roll.

"You know what I mean," he said, a little terse than he meant it to be. Brooke wasn't offended. As you know, she is very attuned to any changes in Rami's mood or manner.

She stopped him but did not let go of his hand. "What do you want to say?"

Rami looked down at the ground in thought.

He paused for a second but then just said it: "You're welcome here." He hesitated to look back up at her. But when he did, she greeted him with a smile that said she was proud of him. He smiled back at her.

"Can we?" he asked.

"I don't know. Where do we put them? The barn?!" She laughed.

Rami didn't laugh. He had considered the idea that more people may show up. If Prisha and Bong saw the news about them, surely others did. And god knows that plenty of Americans' lives get canceled out from underneath them.

"Are we putting them in the barn?!" Brooke asked, eyes wide.

"No," Rami said quickly. "I don't know," he corrected himself. "Maybe?"

"Guess it's a good thing Wilson and I cleaned all the shit off the floor," she said with a shrug.

"What was on the floor?" he asked. She hadn't mentioned finding anything when they were cleaning.

"Shit, Rami. Actual. Shit. That's what was on the floor."

Rami burst out laughing. In his entire life, he

had never had anyone actually need to clean actual shit off of anything he owned. Thank god.

"Rami!" someone at the gate started yelling at him. The other joined in, waving and shouting his name.

"Mr. Popular," Brooke said, teasing him.

"Shut up," he said, trying not to laugh.

When they reached the gate, Rami realized that it didn't make sense for him to say, "Hi, I'm Rami," since they all seemed to know who he was.

So instead, he said, "Hi folks! I imagine..." he trailed off. Everyone waited for him to finish his sentence. He didn't.

Brooke looked at him, confused. Did you have a stroke? she thought. But he didn't look back at her. His eyes stayed fixed at a point out in the distance. She looked to where he was fixated.

That's when she saw the dirt kicking up down the road. Which meant trucks. And she would only have to wait maybe five seconds before she could see the headlights.

Four trucks headed their way. And she recognized all of them.

"Oh boy..." Rami said.

The people at the gate stood quietly and confused.

The first truck pulled up about 50 feet from the gate. The following two trucks flanked the first. The last truck, Dickie's, once again didn't stop in time and ran past Ralph's truck, almost hitting one of the cars parked in front of the gate.

Ralph Elmore jumped out of the first truck. Rayray got out of his truck just as quickly and went over to Ray's truck, where Ray stayed behind the wheel, the engine still running. Dickie hopped out of his vehicle and started walking over to Ralph. Bart jumped out of Dickie's truck and wandered towards the gate. His curiosity compelled him toward the fence.

Now - here's a wild moment that nobody saw coming:

As Bart scanned the people at the gate, he caught Rami's eye. And held it. The two of them seemed frozen, looking into each other's eyes.

Rami felt a sensation he couldn't recognize at first.

Bart did recognize the sensation. It felt the way it does when he swings by the gas station and Ron is working in the garage. He still didn't know what it meant. But he knew he didn't want to stop looking at Rami.

"What's going on, Ralph?" Rami finally called out to the trucks.

"We want to ask you the same thing," Ralph said. He looked around at the strangers on his side of the gate. "But it looks pretty evident."

The strangers looked at each other and then back at Rami.

Brooke turned to Rami to see what he planned to do.

Ralph took a few steps closer to the gate, his gaze also on Rami.

All eyes focused on Rami.

Rami looked around, took a deep breath, and spoke.

EXITLUDE

We'll need to get out of here fairly soon, so we should start heading back to the car.

But I want to point out that Ralph is standing in the exact spot he stood in when he went to confront Rami that first time.

Obviously, as you can see from all the trucks and portapotties around us, that wasn't the last time Ralph confronted Rami.

However, this time will be Ralph's last.

After today, Ralph will have one more conversation with Rami, but it will be very different from all their previous conversations.

And here's why: a car will be pulling up soon - very soon, in fact - and Ralph is clueless that it's coming.

This is the same car that left Boise, Idaho, some

eleven hours, twenty-eight minutes, and thirty-nine seconds ago.

Here's the conversation the driver of said vehicle just had about fifteen or twenty minutes ago:

"Do you know where the farmhouse is?"

"The one up..." Gerry started to reply before being cut off.

"What other fucking farmhouse could I possibly be talking about? Are you inbred?"

Gerry took offense to this - but felt the situation was more volatile than he had first read and did not want to be the one to light the fuse. Without another word, he grabbed a pen and pulled some receipt paper out of the register. He could write the directions by heart; he'd given them out so many times over the last year. He thrust the piece of paper out and started to say, "It's pretty easy to get to," but the bell on the door cut him off as it rang to let him know that he was once again alone.

He didn't know who he had just spoken with. But they didn't seem like someone interested in moving into that house. Even though that's where they were headed. They just didn't seem like one of the shametowners. That's what the locals started calling the ranch residents.

Shametowners could be identified by their unease in public and the way they didn't want to make eye contact with you. They exuded a nervousness that every one of them - at least the ones who stopped by the gas station - seemed to be controlled by.

The whirlwind of vitriol just shouted at him was not nervous. In any way. Even a little. A mission blazed with fury behind those eyes. A purpose. A goal.

A destination.

The farmhouse.

Like so many others.

Okay - let's start driving towards that little elevated area a few yards away from the crowd. We'll be able to see the fireworks fly without getting caught in the ensuing conflagration.

Do you see over near Dickie's truck - Rayray is looking at his phone. That's because a call is coming in. But not from a number he recognizes.

The phone number appearing on his caller ID is the gas station's, and the caller is Gerry. But Rayray never had reason to call the gas station, and thus no reason to save the number to his phone. So that's why he is looking at the phone ringing, deciding if he should answer it.

Now, Rayray is similar to me in this regard and will simply decline the call. If you don't know who's calling - let it go to voicemail. If they don't leave a voicemail, it clearly isn't that important.

Ralph is going to wish that Rayray did answer that call. It would have given him at least a little time to prepare. But Rayray isn't going to listen to the voicemail for another 3 minutes, and by that time, Ralph will already be watching the dust cloud kicking up down the road.

Ralph knows that only one thing causes a dust cloud like the one holding his attention at this moment: a truck.

He doesn't have anyone out running errands. Dickie and Bart just returned with a whole bunch of food and water.

He just scanned the area. You can see just as well as Ralph - all of the trucks owned by the people he knows are present and accounted for.

This truck is a surprise. He doesn't know who is coming his way. And Ralph is unsettled by this fact.

As you know, Ralph is a paranoid man, and not knowing what is about to happen is a sure-fire way to trigger his paranoia. So, as you can assume, Ralph is in a state of paranoia from being triggered by the mystery truck barreling towards the farmhouse.

The good news for us is that when Ralph is paranoid he becomes irritable, and when he's irritable, he tends to yell. His yelling forces others to yell, and there you have it: we're able to hear the whole hullabaloo from the comfort of our car.

With the windows rolled down, of course.

"Rayray! You got those binoculars in your truck?"

"Sure thing!"

It looks like Rayray is running over to his truck to grab them.

Now watch Ralph's face as he looks through the lenses. You've heard how people turn green with seasickness? You're about to watch it happen to Ralph while standing on solid ground.

"Oh fuck."

There he goes. Like a pale pea soup. Makes you sorta nauseous yourself. Like when someone near you vomits.

"Everything okay?"

Rayray is going to wait a long time if he's expecting a response from Ralph.

Ralph has no answer. He doesn't know how to answer. He doesn't even know what he will say in about 2 minutes when he has to say something.

Here is what is currently running through Ralph's head: Fuck, fuck, fuck, fuck, FUCK!

This part is a little sad. Even if Ralph is an asshole. For the next 30 seconds or so, he's going to pace in random directions trying to decide what to do next - as if his choice is behind Door One, Two, or Three, and he isn't sure which one to open.

Ralph is not a coward though. And he will decide that the best thing to do is turn around and face the music. "Take it like a man," as his abusive father used to scream at him while turning his backside black and blue with a heavy leather belt.

Ralph is currently thinking, Take it like a man. "Take it like a man."

He didn't mean to say that out loud. Which is why he just quickly looked around him to see if anyone was nearby and heard him.

And now, keep your eyes on that truck, pulling up about 10 feet from Ralph.

The crowd is going to slowly move towards Ralph and gather near the vehicle that just arrived. Ralph is not aware of this gathering. He's too busy trying to figure out what the fuck he is going to do.

This is where you get to see Ralph really sweat. Nobody is going to get out of that truck for about 40 seconds, the engine still running. Just long enough to wind up Ralph's anxiety but not long enough that anyone approaches the vehicle.

As you can see, the windows were tinted. So while Ralph knows who hurled that dust cloud up behind them, nobody else can see into the cab.

The anticipation is killing Ralph.

Right now, Ralph is thinking, this is to make me sweat.

He is correct. This is absolutely to make him sweat.

And once the driver of the mystery vehicle feels that Ralph has sweated enough, they'll turn off the ignition and kill the engine.

And there you have it: silence settling over the entire field. It seems even the birds have taken the hint and stopped singing.

You see the driver's side door opening? That giant, mean-looking woman hopping out, ripping her sunglasses off her face, and throwing them at Ralph is about to offer up a criticism of Ralph that she's put great thought into during the entirety of her journey: "You dumb fuck!"

Everyone is looking at Ralph right now because nobody knows who this woman is. But she clearly knows him. And he seems to know her, even though his body language indicates he wishes he didn't.

Here's where her flair for the dramatic is truly on display. She's about to walk over to the front passenger seat and open the door with a snappy, almost biting, flourish.

Ralph's heart is racing.

It's nowhere close to how fast it will be racing in just a moment when a backpack flies out and lands on the ground.

He doesn't want to see any of this. So while everyone around him leans in to see better, he's going to do his best to turn invisible or evaporate from our planet's history altogether.

Here's the thing: he knew this day was coming. He's known for a while. He knew it would be bad. Worse than bad. Life upending.

And it is. And it will be.

Alright, ready to watch the minds of Ralph's friends, family and allies brains get blown while Ralph's life crashes down around him?

It's faint, but you can hear a small grunt coming from inside the truck. That's the sound of someone shimmying over to the door when their kids' size eight shoes don't touch the floor.

And that is in fact a child who just leapt out onto the grass, about 8 feet from Ralph.

Things are about to get weird and intense, so we should start heading out of here. But don't worry - this is the moment this beast of a woman has been waiting for - her entire reason for making this drive. So she's going to be loud enough for us to hear, even over the sound of dirt and gravel, when she paralyzes Ralph with a stare and shouts:

"Meet your daddy, Tucker!"

NEXT TIME...

Well, now you know where things stand. As I hoped you would.

You'll be glad we got out of there when we did. Once the trucks start leaving, the mud will make it impossible for a sedan to get through without getting stuck. Believe me - once the other guys figure out precisely what is going on with Ralph and the Beast Woman, they are going to get out while the gettings' good. In about 2 minutes, the only people standing at the gate will be Ralph, the Mulfords, Tucker, and his mama.

And Wally Combs, of course. Who just stumbled on the next biggest story since the barricade at the gate.

Ralph will be sorry he's been speaking to the press so much these past few months. Ralph will be particularly sorry he spoke to Wally instead of having the guys remove him when he had the chance, especially when tomorrow's headline in the Billings Gazette reads "Shametown Shamer Shamed" in bold letters above a photo of Ralph.

As I'm sure you've gathered, there is so much more to this story. The saga has only just begun, and I promise that everyone touched by these events will be forever changed. And just like the good Doc told Wilson - none of them have any clue what comes next.

I'll pick you up next time - I do appreciate the ride to the gate, though; my car would never have made it. So, as a sign of my gratitude, I'll use this remaining time to give you a taste of what I'll show you when we meet up again:

Last we left Rami and the farmhouse family; he and Brooke were at the gate addressing the folks looking for a place to stay. Or at least, they were about to address them when Ralph and his crew pulled up as noisily and dustily as possible. And here we are: Rami and Ralph facing off on either side of the fence. But let's back up a bit:

"What's going on, Ralph?" Rami finally called out to the trucks.

"We want to ask you the same thing," Ralph said. He looked around at the strangers on his side of the gate. "But it looks pretty evident."

The strangers looked at each other and then back at Rami.

Brooke turned to Rami to see what he planned to do.

Ralph took a few steps closer to the gate, his gaze also on Rami.

All eyes focused on Rami.

Rami looked around, took a deep breath, and spoke.

"I'm sorry, but there is no room for you here!"

Brooke's shocked expression matches the disappointed look on the gate-gatherers' faces.

"Rami!" Brooke starts before he cuts her off.

"I wish we could help you, but there are no more rooms in the..."

"We're happy to camp out!" one of the voices at the gate interrupted before other voices joined in agreement.

"I understand that..." Rami tries to shout over the chorus of people assuring him they love sleeping under the stars.

This is not how this was supposed to go. Again. Like always.

His introverted nature started taking over as his social capital was drained rapidly. He needed help.

He needed help.

And then the answer struck him.

Will Brooke understand? he asked himself as he watched her pained expression from the corner of his eye.

Don't really have a choice in the matter, do I?

He didn't.

Stop! You can let me off here. Again, the ride is much appreciated! But before you drive off, let me finish telling you what Rami did:

He said the one thing that would silence everyone - and I mean everyone:

"Please leave now, or I will ask my friends Ralph and Rayray here to remove you from the property!" Rami shouted, gesturing to a flabbergasted Ralph.

Didn't see that one coming, did you?

ANDREW HOBGOOD is a playwright, author, and director based in Chicago and Milwaukee. He is the founder of The New Colony in Chicago, a non-profit theater company dedicated to supporting new playwrights and artists in creating new works. Hobgood has written and directed numerous plays throughout his career, including "5 Lesbians Eating a Quiche," which ran Off-Broadway and is published with Concord Theatricals. Hobgood has been a tireless advocate for emerging artists, and his commitment to supporting new voices in the theater world has earned him widespread recognition and acclaim. He has been featured in numerous publications, including the Chicago Tribune and Time Out Chicago, and has received awards for his work, including Outstanding Production at FringeNYC. He currently lives in Milwaukee with his partner Joe and their dog Wyatt and is enjoying taking in all the cheese curds and craft brews.

AndyWritesThings.com